MURDER at YAQUINA HEAD

PRAISE FOR *MURDER AT YAQUINA HEAD*

"When an elderly friend of Thomas Martindale is found murdered, the vacationing journalism professor and amateur sleuth turns to a manuscript—a WWII memoir of her youth in occupied France—the woman had given him. [The novel] follows the sardonic Martindale as he prowls the Oregon coast on the trail of former Nazis." — *Publishers Weekly*

". . . Mixed with details of a lighthouse, the Oregon coast, and an aquarium, this is all good stuff for a mystery. What really makes it a good read, however, is the self-effacing Martindale, a delightful if sometimes exasperating sleuth who is far too nosy for his own good. . . . He never seems to understand that he could be in danger." — *Denver Post*

Former journalism professor and Oregon native Lovell debuts a series featuring an Oregonian journalism professor. Not much of a stretch, but Lovell's firsthand knowledge lends an air of credibility to the story and the setting. Tom Martindale has just begun his summer vacation on the Oregon coast when his charming French professor friend, Simone Godard, asks him to read her manuscript. She confides in Tom that her life may be in danger, but she's murdered before she can elaborate. Tom looks for clues in the manuscript, which details Simone's participation in the French Resistance movement during World War II. Although [Lovell] at times underestimates the reader's detecting ability by dropping obvious plot hints, he crafts a convincing story peppered with absorbing details about World War II. Much of the fun here is reading Simone's gripping memoir over Tom's shoulder. — *Booklist*

Set on the windswept Oregon coast and capably written by Oregon resident Ron Lovell, *Murder at Yaquina Head* is the riveting story of journalism professor Thomas Martindale, a man who becomes drawn into a tangle of deceit and death when his friend's life is endangered and he discovers a murdered body. Wry, thoughtful, moody, and structured around a secret that reaches back to the era of World War II, *Murder at Yaquina Head* is a . . . gripping mystery which is highly recommended for mystery buffs and would make a welcome and appreciated addition to any community library. — *The Bookwatch*

A Thomas Martindale Mystery

MURDER at YAQUINA HEAD

Ron Lovell

A Penman Productions Book

THIRD EDITION

Penman Productions, Gleneden Beach, Oregon

Copyright © 2010 by Ronald P. Lovell

First Edition published by Sunstone Press, 2002

Second edition published by Penman Productions, 2006

The events, people, and incidents in this story are the sole product
of the author's imagination. The story is fictional and any resemblance
to individuals living or dead is purely coincidental.

Printed in the United States of America

Library of Congress Control Number: 2006900713

ISBN: 978-0-9767978-1-4

Cover and book designer: Liz Kingslien

Editor: Mardelle Kunz

Cover photo: Dave Nishitani

Author photo: Dennis Wolverton

*Those who do not remember the past are condemned
to relive it. — George Santayana*

Saturday

Adam, you're just plain stupid if you think I pay you to come up here to gawk at seagulls. I guess you are plain stupid, aren't you? You're an idiot, but I'm a bigger idiot for putting up with your shit."

"Momma says you're not supposed to say bad words like that."

"Hell, I'm not interested in what your mama has to say. You're a grown man with a job. But it's a job you won't have much longer if you continue to fuck with me, Adam. I'm warning you."

"Momma says that's an even worser word to say. She says we don't say words like fuck."

I tried to ignore this altercation as I walked to the edge of the deck and paused to read the plaques. One gave a brief history of the building behind me—the Yaquina Head Lighthouse. Its recent reopening by the Bureau of Land Management meant that visitors could now climb to the top. I didn't plan to make that effort today because of the fog.

I turned and looked up at the tall stone tower. Puffs of vapor swirled around its curved sides, sometimes obscuring the top, sometimes allowing me to see it clearly. A moment like this epitomized for me the mysterious and magical role lighthouses play in the scheme of things. They are both protectors and seducers, warning of dangerous rocks while at the same time beckoning the unwary mariner toward them.

The cold, clammy shroud of fog penetrated my clothes and made me shiver as I read the next plaque, this one about the various birds and seals inhabiting the rocks below and the sky above me. I could hear seals barking in the distance, but hadn't seen any birds although the ugly white splotches randomly deposited on the deck's wooden planks gave evidence that those feathered—and diarrhea-prone—creatures were nearby. I smiled as I thought about the T-shirt sold at local shops: dark blue, appropriate white splatter, and the words "I Hate Seagulls." Except for someone spitting in your face, nothing is as degrading as being the victim of such a direct hit.

Then I heard the same two voices again.

"I've had it with you, Adam. If you don't get your act together, I'm going to fire you. I can promise you that."

"Momma says people shouldn't break promises."

Because fog distorts sound as well as sight, I didn't hear everything the man said in reply.

"Arrggrr . . . impossible . . . you . . . an idiot."

I could tell that one of the two was getting angrier by the minute as his voice got louder and his words harsher, even though I couldn't see him. Soon, he walked off in the opposite direction, the loud thud of his shoes reverberating on the boards and against the ephemeral walls of the fog bank. I continued to read the legend in front of me, but soon felt the presence of someone to my left. It had to be the one called Adam.

I turned, expecting to see a gawky teenager with acne and spiked hair. Instead, there stood a tall and slender man with curly brown hair and fine features, probably in his thirties. In his red-checkered shirt and yellow rain slicker, he could be a model for an ad selling fish fillets or extolling the benefits of ocean conservation.

"You like birds?" he asked, smiling broadly.

"Well, yes, I do."

"I do, too. I like it here best. This is my best place in the world."

Saying that, the fresh-faced young man turned and disappeared into the fog that enveloped him quickly, making me wonder if he had been there at all. The man, the fog, the deafening stillness—it all combined to make me feel uncomfortable enough to get out of there as quickly as I could.

I t didn't take long to reach my house, about a mile from the lighthouse. I was eager to settle in and start my vacation, which meant three months away from my duties teaching journalism at Oregon University. I had recently bought this house on a cliff above the sea just north of Newport and planned to spend the summer here reading and working on several writing projects.

I was carrying the last box of books from my car to the house when my cell phone rang. All phone calls are an interruption, but this insistent trill seemed particularly annoying on a day when I hoped I had left such distractions behind on campus. I placed the box on a table, picked up the phone, and punched the answer button.

"Hello."

"*Bonjour*, Tom."

"*Bonjour*, Simone. Good to hear your voice."

I had known Simone Godard for ten years. She was a well-established professor of French at the university and I a mid-career associate professor of journalism when we first met on a committee.

In the years since, we had kept in touch periodically, she more diligently than I. Simone was a terrible flirt, and I enjoyed sparring back and forth about a liaison we both knew would never happen. We weren't really interested in one another romantically. She was, after all, thirty-five years older, although she didn't look it.

I hadn't heard much from her since her retirement three years ago. After she read in the faculty newsletter that I had gotten a research grant to support my writing this summer—and that I would be doing the writing at my small house on the Oregon coast—she had written me a note asking to see me.

"Is this a good time to talk, Thomas? Am I interrupting?"

"Any call from you is never an interruption."

I often said innocuous things like that, but with Simone, I meant it.

"You are always so kind, Thomas, if perhaps a little insincere, eh?"

"I'm just bringing the last boxes in from the car and getting settled."

"I very much want to see you and show you something I've written. I read it to my literary group, but I want to see what you think of it."

"That sounds intriguing. Tell me more."

"It's all about my years in the French Resistance. I was just a girl, really, when I got involved. I delivered a clandestine newspaper right under the noses of the Germans in our little town. Later, in Paris, I helped get American pilots out of the country."

"Simone, I had no idea you were such a heroine. I would be honored to read what you've written. A short piece or a whole book?"

"It's a full-length memoir of my life, Thomas. As I've gotten older, it's become important for me to clear the air about certain things. Writing this has been very cathartic for me. I've just got to get some of the events in my life down on paper."

"I'll have a lot of time before I start my own writing this summer."

"Come to a brunch I'm having, and I'll give you a copy."

"I'll be there. When and where?"

"At my home tomorrow at ten. Just a few friends and colleagues. I'd love you to join us. I live in Depoe Bay on Point Avenue—a large gray house on the cliff above the sea. Turn off Highway 101 on South Point Street."

"I'll find it."

"And *cheri?*"

"Yes, Simone?"

"I need to consult with you about another matter: I think someone may be following me to do me harm. See you tomorrow, *mon ami.*"

Before I could ask her more, she hung up. I considered calling her back, but decided she hadn't sounded distressed. I would probably know all about this soon enough.

I made one last trip to the car to make sure I had everything, then parked it in the carport. I walked back into the house and closed and locked the door.

This would be my first extended stay since I bought the house six months ago. I was familiar with it, however, because I had rented it ten years earlier while on sabbatical leave. My then landlord—a history professor—had just taken another job in the East and agreed to sell it. I scraped together half the purchase price, and he was carrying a contract on the balance.

Buying this house was the fulfillment of a long-held dream to live near the ocean. Even when I returned in the fall to teach classes sixty miles away, I would be close enough to spend every weekend here.

I accomplished a lot that evening and felt good about being settled in when I went to bed.

Sunday

Simone's directions were easy to follow, and I rolled up to her house the following morning with ten minutes to spare. The house was huge: two stories with all kinds of towers, eaves, and dormer windows. I could hear, but not see, the ocean as it crashed against the rocks below the cliff at the rear.

She must have been watching for me because she opened the front door before I knocked. She looked great in a silk caftan, tailored to emphasize her trim figure. Even though she was in her seventies, she looked twenty years younger.

"*Bonjour, cheri.* So good to see my favorite man."

She kissed me on both cheeks and led me into a foyer where I caught a glimpse of the room beyond. It had a beamed ceiling two stories high and windows with a spectacular view of the sea and sky.

"Wow, Simone. This is something. I had no idea. I mean, the house. It's so big and . . . "

"Expensive? I got a generous divorce settlement many years ago and invested the money well. I also inherited money from my brother when he died. Then I have my retirement from the university, of course. I live comfortably. Come and meet my other guests."

"No, no, Simone. I meant to say big and beautiful . . . breathtaking. That describes you, too. Except for the word big," I laughed.

"Oh, Tom, you delightful flirt."

She led me down several steps and as we entered, people who were gathered in groups turned toward us.

"Everyone, this is my dear friend Thomas Martindale." Then she guided me to her other guests.

"This is Connie Wright, a friend and fellow board member of the local symphony." A short, slightly overweight woman with expensive clothes, too much makeup, and big, platinum hair smiled and took my outstretched hand. She looked fifty trying to be thirty.

"Who is this, Simone? Another handsome man from your past? You must have an endless supply." She laughed, looked me up and down, then fixed her eyes on my left hand. "And where is Mrs. Martin . . . "

" . . . dale. Martindale. It's English."

"Martin-dale. Yes. How stupid of me. Your wife? Is she with you?"

"There is no Mrs. Martindale. I'm not married."

"Ohhhh. How thrilling." She grabbed my arm and squeezed it tightly, the bracelets on her wrist jingling wildly. Simone had to gently pry her fingers loose so we could move on.

"Tom, this is Verne Andrews."

A big, beefy man of about sixty stuck out his hand. He wore his white hair in a ponytail and had a mustache and goatee combination that looked theatrical. He was dressed better than most people who live at the coast, but still conveyed that white belt, loud plaid, small town chamber of commerce, slap-on-the-back, forced friendliness of good ol' boys doing business. The other distinctive thing was a large turquoise clasp holding his bolo tie.

"Great to meet you, by golly. Any friend of See-moan is a friend of mine." Her name rolled around on his tongue before he managed to get the word out.

"Verne's a friend and my attorney."

Now it was Simone's turn to ward off advances. She deftly ducked out from under the massive arm he tried to put around her. She smiled and moved me to the next group.

"This is Stacy Thomas. She's a former student who lives in the area and helps me with my research."

A pretty young woman with a bright smile and flowing blond hair turned to face me. As she held out her hand, the young man next to her glared at me as if I were some kind of rival. For a moment, I thought he might even step between us. What was there for him to be jealous of? She introduced him as Joe George. I smiled, shook his hand, and followed Simone to a gray-blond man with piercing cold eyes, who snapped his heels together and straightened his shoulders as he grasped my hand.

"Manfred Bader," he said, a slight smile on his face. "I've heard your name on campus for years, but we've never met."

"And I yours, Mr. Bader."

"Fred, please. I go by that."

"Fred is a colleague who teaches German. We've kept in touch because of . . . mutual interests," added Simone.

"My wife, Elaine."

The small woman standing slightly behind him looked mousy—thick glasses, no makeup, a shapeless brown suit covering her thin frame. She was the kind of person who melted into the background in the presence of strikingly beautiful women like Simone and Stacy.

"Good morning, Mrs. Bader."

Her return smile was hesitant and fleeting.

Simone moved me to a side table where she picked up a glass of champagne and offered it to me.

"To absent friends," she said, raising her glass to the group.

We all responded. While I am no expert, it tasted good

and immediately sent a slightly woozy message from my empty stomach to my head. Connie Wright moved between the Baders and placed her arm through his, a move his wife seemed not to notice. A woman in a gray uniform and white apron appeared at the top of the steps.

"Brunch is served, mad-dame." This French pronunciation was giving the locals a hard time.

"Thank you, Rose. We'll be right in."

She turned to me. "Rose Edwards, my cook and house-keeper. I'll introduce you later," she said, as she took my arm and pulled me across the room. "Come on, my dears. Let's eat."

As we sat down, Connie Wright injected herself between Simone and me, much to my chagrin. Elaine Bader was sitting on my other side. The table was set with exquisite china— Limoges, no doubt—and covered with a linen tablecloth. At each place was a starched napkin held in place by a silver ring crested with a fleur-de-lis. A gold-trimmed vase in the center held yellow roses. The cook soon emerged from a door at the end of the room carrying a large platter of crêpes. She served several to each of us.

"You can fill them with anything from the chafing dishes," said Simone, waving toward the center of the table. "There's fruit, eggs, bacon. *Bon appetit*, everyone."

Table talk covered the usual subjects as we ate—the weather, politics, living on the coast. Every time I tried to talk with Mrs. Bader, she half turned her back to me as if to ward off any conversation. Rebuffed in that direction, I was forced to give Connie more attention than I would have preferred.

"Simone tells me you're a writer, Tom."

"Yes, that's right. I teach writing and try to practice what I teach."

"That's wonderful. I've never met a writer before. It must be . . . so . . . interesting." As she spoke, she turned her face toward me and opened and closed her heavily-mascaraed eyes. I did my best to deflect her interest.

"Simone. You really look good. Truly ageless." As I spoke, Connie smoothed her hair and readjusted her tight-fitting dress, as if I were talking to her.

"I try, *cheri*," said Simone. "Luckily, I've never had a weight problem. I can eat anything I want and not gain a pound."

When Simone said that, Connie dropped her fork so quickly it fell to the floor. I started to retrieve it, but she stopped me. "Excuse me, please." I got up and pulled out her chair, and she practically ran from the room. What had we said to upset her? I was baffled, but Simone and I resumed our conversation immediately.

"Did you know I was starving when the war ended?"

I swallowed my last bite before I replied. "No, you've never mentioned your wartime experiences until yesterday. You said you were in the French Resistance."

She nodded and sipped her champagne. "A part of my impetuous youth, I fear. Yes, I was involved with the Underground." She leaned closer, her voice dropping to a whisper. "That's what I have written about. That's why I think . . ."

"What are you two talking about in such conspiratorial tones?" Fred Bader was trying to join our conversation from halfway down the table.

"Only idle chitchat, Fred. If we are finished, let's move to the salon for coffee and pastry. I made it myself."

I got up to pull out her chair, but Verne Andrews beat me to it.

"There you are, little lady. By golly," he said, "that was a mighty good ree-past."

Bader suddenly appeared at my side. "Forgive me, Tom. Or

should I call you Professor Martindale? In my native country, the title professor really means something."

"No, no. Tom is good, Fred."

"Did I hear Simone say something about consulting you about her writing? I hadn't known of your expertise in reviewing texts in French."

He apparently didn't know about her memoir. The little voice that sometimes keeps me from revealing things that had best be kept secret kicked in before I answered. "I only know a little French. I think she wants me to . . . to look at her manuscript to see if it has the usual stuff for texts—study questions, chapter summaries, that kind of thing. I've written some journalism books, so I guess she thinks I can help her. We haven't really discussed it at length."

We parted as we reached the windows where everyone was looking out at the ocean. Spray and foam from the waves below were sprinkling the glass. That old jerk Verne Andrews was talking to Simone.

" . . . want to sell it, I know I can get a good price for you."

"Why would I part with this jewel of a place? I love it and plan to spend the rest of my days right here."

Verne looked disappointed.

"I'm sorry we didn't get to know one another better." Stacy Thomas was standing next to me—minus the jealous boyfriend, who had gone off to tone his muscles or something.

"I . . . er . . . well, yes. It would have been fun to talk. You helped Simone with her book?"

"Stace!" Joe George, all two hundred pounds of rippling muscles, came rushing across the room. He grabbed Stacy's arm and pulled her toward him. "We'd better be goin', don't you think?"

"I was just talking to Tom, Joe. I'm not ready to go anywhere just now. If you want to leave, go ahead. I'm sure Tom can give me a ride."

George's face reddened and the muscles in his neck tightened. Was every woman in this part of the coast as forward as Stacy and Connie?

"I'm afraid I'll be staying a while," I replied, putting my hands up in mock defense against both Stacy and Joe.

"Oh, sure. You really know how to hurt a girl," she laughed. She looked up at George and kissed him hard. "Come on, handsome. Let's split." Whatever anger he felt toward her—or me—seemed to evaporate. They walked arm-in-arm across the room and out the front door.

The five who remained sat around for another hour or so. Then I caught a glance at my watch and was alarmed to see that it was 3 P.M. I had a lot more work to do yet, like setting up my computer and shopping for groceries.

"I really need to go, Simone."

"Oh, *cheri*, must you?"

I nodded, a mock sadness on my face.

"Let me get you my manuscript."

"Oh, yes, the textbook," I said, glancing at Fred Bader, who was listening.

Simone immediately understood. "I hope you'll be able to help me with it."

She disappeared into a room next to the salon that was lined with bookshelves—I suppose her study. She reappeared carrying a brown envelope labeled "Basic French Text" in large letters. Simone made sure Bader saw the inscription as she passed the package to me.

"I'll walk out with you, Thomas," she said, as we crossed the room.

"Great to meet all of you," I shouted over my shoulder as

we departed. Connie suddenly reappeared in the living room, looking as though she had reapplied her mascara. She glanced at me, then abruptly turned her back and walked toward Verne Andrews. I saw her batting her eyes at him and smiling broadly, her bracelets jingling loudly. Simone propelled me through the door, and I didn't speak until we got to my car.

"We didn't get to talk about your being followed. I didn't think you wanted to bring it up in front of the others."

"You were so right, *mon ami*, especially Fred Bader. I think he's . . . let's just say he may have ulterior motives in his friendship with me."

"What do you mean, ulterior motives?"

"I don't want to answer until you've read this. It may be why someone is following me. I guess I need to modify that—why someone may be trying to kill me."

"Kill you! What hap . . ."

"Madame Godard." It was Rose Edwards, her cook, shouting from a door at the end of the house. "I'm sorry to interrupt, but it's Adam. He's come back and he's in trouble. Can you talk to him?"

"Of course, Rose. I'll be right there." She turned to me. "Her son is somewhat retarded. He's a grown man, but talks like an eight year old. He gets into scrapes once in a while. I help him when he does." As she turned toward the house, she said, "Call me when you've read this, and I'll tell you everything. *Au revoir*, Tom."

I watched as a man joined her and Rose outside the door. Simone embraced them both and they went inside. From where I was standing, Rose Edwards's son looked like the man I had encountered the day before at the lighthouse. As I recalled, the man who had been so angry had called him Adam.

I walked to my car and started the engine. As I drove out of the turnaround, I noticed Fred Bader watching me from the doorway.

3

L ater that night, I sat down in my most comfortable chair and opened the envelope. Simone had placed a Post-it note on the first page of the manuscript.

"If someone wants me dead," it read, "this is the reason why." I turned the page and started reading.

Murders in Wartime
by Simone Godard

I was not raised to be a heroine. My childhood in the small fishing village of Le Croisic was quite ordinary, except that I lived in what my friends called a castle. It wasn't that at all, of course, but the lighthouse on Pointe du Croisic on the Bay of Biscay where my father was the keeper. And I didn't actually live in the lighthouse, but in a small cottage up the hill from it.

But my friends and I played in the tower all the time, and I usually made myself a princess and wore an old chiffon dress I took from my mother's rag bag. The neighborhood boys in our group, including my brother, were knights who put on cardboard armor to look their parts.

I loved that lighthouse all of my life and was very proud of my father's role in keeping ships from crashing on the rocky shores at its base.

The idyll of my youth came to an abrupt halt on September 3, 1939, when the French government declared war on Germany. After eight months of la drôle de guerre—*phony war*—a period when nothing happened on either side, Germany invaded France on May 10, 1940. The French army was defeated in six weeks.

On June 22, Marshal Philippe Pétain, a French hero in World War I and leader of our armed forces, signed an armistice with the Germans and became head of state of the slightly less than half of the country the Germans did not occupy. He established his headquarters in Vichy, a spa town in central France noted for its hot springs and mineral water. The Nazis occupied most of the north and west, which included the industrial wealth and a majority of the population.

Although Pétain pledged what he called "honorable" collaboration with the Germans, he and his government quickly became tools of the Nazis and yielded to them on almost every issue, getting very little in return. When the Allies invaded North Africa in November 1942, Hitler annulled the armistice he had signed with Pétain and occupied the part of France he didn't already hold.

When France fell in 1940, I was fifteen and attending lycee in Le Croisic. This was in a part of the country occupied immediately by the Germans—a region called Brittany. Our village was twenty-five kilometers from the shipbuilding town of Saint Nazaire and about four hundred kilometers southwest of Paris.

The need for my family and friends to become daring and heroic came in June of 1940, when, from his exile in London, General Charles de Gaulle called for us to resist the Germans. It took a while for the formal organization that came to be called the Resistance to be set up, so in the meantime I joined a Catholic group with similar goals. We were a group of about twelve people—mostly girls—and we published a newspaper from the hidden cellar of a photographer's shop. I never actually saw the press because I was one of two who distributed the paper after it had been printed. There was no need for me to go into the cellar. Our leader was the local barber.

It was a primitive publication, printed on two sides of one sheet. It came out once a week and contained whatever news we could get our hands on. At first, it was hard to get any information because the Germans had confiscated all shortwave radios. Eventually my father, who tinkered with radios as a hobby, built one we hid in a hole in our cellar floor. Finally, we were able to hear BBC broadcasts.

Someone would bring me the papers in a bundle, and I would go out on foot at about three in the morning and leave copies in the mail slots of houses. As I made the rounds in the village, I strained to listen for German patrols. I shoved the folded papers through the tiny openings, being careful not to let the flaps snap back because even the smallest sound would carry in the quiet night. Fortunately for me, the patrols made a lot of noise. The clunk, clunk, clunk of the half-track treads reverberated from blocks away. I could easily duck out of sight when I heard one approaching.

So full of foolish bravado was I that I sometimes followed the vehicles after they had gone by, just out of sight—at least I hoped I was out of sight—almost daring them to see me and challenge my presence at so early an hour. How foolish I was. How impetuous.

Very few people in town were interested in the French Resistance. In fact, our town was full of collaborators. I think most people were happy the war was over for France. Also, you have to remember, the Germans behaved themselves. After the first week, though, troops looted the homes of the wealthy. One man resisted and the Germans shot him on the spot. They left his body in the street a whole week as a reminder to everybody else about what happened to people who didn't cooperate.

One day the Germans burst into the cellar and found the girls with the printing press and sent them to Auschwitz. Strangely enough, the photographer was not arrested. I guess he convinced the Germans that he did not know the press was in the cellar.

I was not picked up, but the barber was. He jumped from a train into a river while he was being transported to a concentration camp. He never came back to town.

After I got my degree, I went to Paris to study law at the University of Paris. That was in September 1943. I was also working for a lawyer. As the seat of the German Military Administration, Paris bristled with checkpoints and Nazi insignia. It was a very scary place.

The German occupation of all of France in 1942 forced an increasing number of French resisters and anti-fascists from other countries into hiding. This led to the creation of a formal organization called the Maquis. These resisters needed to be guided to safe places in forests and cellars throughout the country to escape the Gestapo's relentless pursuit. As time went on, the Maquis also turned to guerrilla warfare against German troops by conducting hundreds of incidents of harassment, sabotage, and ambush.

In Paris, I joined one of the Resistance groups. My contact was the nephew of a woman we knew in the country, a man known to me only as Max. As with all such groups, our cell had only three people: me, Max, and one other woman.

The Resistance as a whole consisted of hundreds of cells like ours, concentrating on actions both large—like blowing up a bridge—and small—like publishing clandestine newspapers or helping people who were hunted by the Germans to escape. Although we worked in a common cause, the Resistance was never monolithic. It was not tightly controlled from above. Maybe that's why it was so successful. We did what we could when we could do it without waiting for orders from some unseen hierarchy.

I first made contact with Max via the bulletin board in the lobby of the residence for women where I was living. I was standing at the bulletin board one morning, checking for messages, when I felt the presence of someone next to me.

"Don't look at me, mademoiselle, *but please accompany me to the garden," said a male voice.*

I continued to look at the board, my pulse racing. After a moment, I began to walk as nonchalantly as possible after his departing form. He looked tall and thin, but I couldn't tell much more because of the distance between us. Outside, I caught up with him as he stopped to pick up a beautiful rose petal from the ground. He turned and handed it to me.

"Are you studying botany, Mademoiselle Godard?"

My heart skipped a beat as I looked into his brown eyes. He looked tired, but beyond the gauntness of his face was a handsomeness I had never seen in the gawky boys of my village. His face was ringed with dark hair, partially covered by the kind of cap most male students wore. He grabbed my hand and led me toward a bench.

"Gaze at me amorously, if you will, mademoiselle,*" he whispered. "We are not completely safe from German ears, even outdoors."*

We sat down beside one another, and he leaned over and kissed my neck. I blushed immediately.

"Act as if you are enjoying this," he whispered.

"I will not have to act, monsieur,*" I said, trying to will my red face to return to its natural color.*

"Good. You are blushing, Simone. May I call you Simone?"

I nodded.

"A good thing for a passerby to see."

We began to talk while he turned the petal over in my hand as if he was talking about it. From time to time he nuzzled my neck. I loved the attention and soon forgot to blush.

"I haven't much time, so I must be direct. We in the Resistance are looking for young women like you for important assignments here in Paris. We especially like students because the Germans seem to think you are harmless, and you can move around easily with your student body cards . . . look alive!"

He glanced around and kissed me directly on the mouth as a German officer walked by, a well-dressed, beautiful woman on his arm. He touched his cap at me and smiled before strolling on. Max and I parted, and I suddenly felt the need to straighten my dress and smooth my hair.

"If this is what work in the Resistance is like, I'm ready to serve indefinitely," I said with a straight face.

Max looked at me for a few seconds and then we both started laughing.

Max said he would be in touch whenever he had an assignment for me. My job would be to accompany American and British pilots who had been shot down through the Metro to a point on the outskirts of Paris where someone else would escort them out of the city and, eventually, out of France.

He said each message would say that a package had been received from my family. The package, of course, was a pilot. Our Resistance cell—me, Max, and the girl at the other end who took the pilots to the next station on the route—was typical. We were set up in what was called an infrastructure of anonymity, with the names of participants left unrecorded except at the local level. That way, if one of us was picked up, only three would die. I agreed to join his cell, and we parted with one more kiss. I got my first summons two days later.

I was told to go to the Metro station at 7 P.M. on the day after I received the message, usually a Monday. From that first assignment, the plan went smoothly. Walking arm-in-arm, the pilots and I pretended to be lovers. The pilots were dressed like French peasants, shabby with a growth of beard and hair not combed. There was only one problem: they were too well-fed, too healthy looking.

A month later, as I descended the stairs and walked onto the long platform of one of the largest Metro stations in Paris, there were German troops everywhere, as always; most looked bored as they lounged around, talking to one another in a relaxed way. I walked as nonchalantly as I could to a point down the platform where I would be away from the Germans. I sat on a bench to wait for the next train—and my package. I pretended to be reading one of my law books and soon noticed from the corner of my eye that someone was standing beside me.

As I glanced up, I hoped the look in my eyes would not betray my surprise. Instead of a hearty-looking American pilot, my package on this day was Max himself. With his scruffy beard, gaunt frame, and shabby clothes, he really looked like the French peasant he was supposed to be. I stood up and we embraced.

"Bonjour, mon petit," he said loudly, as he hugged me. "I just dropped a revolver into your bag," he continued in a voice I could barely hear.

"So good to see you, my love," I answered, slinging the bag over my shoulder.

We pretended to chat amiably and amorously as we gazed into each other's eyes and strolled down the platform.

"Same route, same destination," he whispered under the roar of a stopping train. Near the end of the platform, a large group of people stepped from the vehicle and, without another word to me, he joined them as they walked up the stairway to the street above. As quickly as he had appeared, Max had melted into the crowd.

I looked at my watch and made a great show of looking at the schedule posted on the nearest bulletin board. The train that was just pulling out would not take me where I needed to go. I would need to wait for the next one.

Just then, I heard the sound all of us had learned to dread since the German occupation had begun: the ear-splitting trill of an officer's whistle. The troops who had been casual and even slovenly moments before, now snapped to attention and took up positions at the gates, which were slowly being closed. The Germans were about to conduct one of their intermittent sweeps.

As it happened, my bag was full of potatoes, which I had managed to buy earlier in the day—a rare find. As I fell into line behind the people walking slowly toward where the Germans had set up a point to check IDs, I opened the bag and dropped my law book into it. As I did, I shook it once hoping that the wrapped gun would drop to the bottom. I knew I would only have one chance to do this, so I hoped it would work.

"You can't show panic in any way," I said to myself, as I neared my turn at the head of the line and the hard-faced troopers I would need to pass. It took every ounce of self-control not to show the overwhelming fear I felt at that moment. What if I fainted right in front of them?

So far as I could tell, though, no one was paying any attention to me. The officer in charge was pacing back and forth at the bottom of the exit stairs, not looking at anyone but seeming to be angry that this exercise was taking so long.

"Schnell, schnell," he kept shouting, as he snapped the fingers on his right hand. "Schnell."

My heart was beating so fast it was echoing in my ears as I walked toward one of the soldiers. I held the bag open for him and he peered inside hesitantly, as if he expected a snake to materialize and bite him on the nose.

"Schwarzmarket," he said. Black market.

"No," I answered, in as steady a voice as I could muster. "La distribution"—the legal distribution of food. I smiled and looked him directly in the eye, hoping against hope that the officer wouldn't sense a commotion, walk over, and dump the contents of my bag onto the floor.

The soldier considered my words for a moment, then waved me on. I only dared glance at the officer as I scurried past. Before I looked away, I noticed his penetrating green eyes as he glared at everyone around him. Even though I detested everything he stood for, I had to admit that he was very handsome, with an unforgettable face of chiseled features that could well have adorned a propaganda poster extolling the virtues of Hitler's master race.

He didn't seem to notice me as I hurried by. I don't think I exhaled until I was back up on the street. I didn't have time to rest, however, because I was already late for my rendezvous. I walked to the next Metro station on the line, boarded the proper train, and delivered the gun without incident.

The next week I went to my regular meeting with Max. The platform was crowded with the usual mix of French citizens and German soldiers. I sat down on a bench, pulled the law book out of my bag, and pretended to read. For good measure, I made notes in the margins as the good student I was pretending to be. In truth, I was way behind in my studies; my Resistance work was taking its toll on my study time and energy.

I looked up each time the blare of a horn and the clatter of wheels heralded a new train. Max was not on the first one. I kept reading. By the second and third trains, I was really worried and beginning to fear the worst. I quickly left the station and returned to my room.

The plan called for me to go one hour later the next day at the next station and repeat that procedure on the day after that. Max did not come on those days either. That night, a cryptic message was left for me on the bulletin board: "I'm sorry, but we can no longer send you packages. Love, Mother."

The message could mean only one thing: Max had been picked up or forced to go into hiding. Right then, I knew the work of our cell had ended.

Later, just before I went to bed, someone slipped a note under my door saying that Max had been arrested and shot *earlier that day. I cried as I hurriedly packed a few things in a small bag. I kept thinking of his wonderful brown eyes and gentle manner. I remembered our tender moments too, as only a girl who had not known true love can remember even a feigned kiss. I had always hoped that more would develop between us on some distant day when the war was over and we no longer needed to pretend. I crept out of the building after all the lights were out and disappeared into the vastness of Paris. I could not go back to my room for fear the Germans would be waiting for me there. Who knew what Max had revealed under torture? And who could blame him if he did?*

I spent a great deal of time riding the Metro the next day. When they emptied the subways that night, I walked along the tracks and hid in a side tunnel. The next night I slept on a park bench in the freezing rain.

The next day, I caught a bus back to Pointe du Croisic because I felt I would be safer there. By then, March 1944, the French Resistance was operating there in a well-organized way. My job was to listen to the radio—the one my father had made and that we had hidden in an abandoned well in the cellar floor. I learned the messages by heart and carried them to people who waited for me in the woods near our house.

By the messages I was getting, it was clear that troops would be landing on June 6, 1944. At 6 A.M. on that day, I got this message: "The apple trees are in bloom."

"This is it," I said, and ran upstairs and told everyone. "They have landed!"

I listened again at 8 A.M. and the message said that Allied troops had landed at Normandy to the north of us and established a foothold. What a day. We would be rescued soon. Alas, that was not to be.

I kept delivering messages of the same nature for the next week, and then I almost got killed.

At about 10 A.M. on June 12, I was studying for my law exams when I heard the Germans coming in their armored van—clunk, clunk, clunk—with the siren going. I was seized with fear, but then I convinced myself they were arresting other people.

Because of the danger in what we were doing, those of us in the group had decided long ago that we would deny everything if we were ever picked up. Although I had expected to be picked up for some time, I didn't think too much about it. When I joined the Resistance, I had been told, "Chances are, you're not going to get out of this alive." With this thought in mind, we had been preparing our story, mother and I. We rehearsed it several times.

The van clattered to a stop in front of our house and a driver, a captain, and three soldiers got out. All of them but the officer carried machine guns. The soldiers guarded both doors, and the captain came in with his pistol drawn, followed by one of the soldiers. It looked very bad for us as we stood facing him.

"We have information that you are working for the Underground," the captain said. "This is a real nest of the Underground, and we are going to clean it up. You are under arrest."

Then he pulled out papers that said we had been condemned to death. Everyone was listed on it: my father, my mother, my brother, and I. It was printed very neatly. Someone had obviously turned us in.

They knew all about our radio and that I delivered messages. What they didn't know was that my father had for some time gone to the sites of crashed planes and picked up weapons and ammunition that he was stashing in the attic and in the cellar of the lighthouse, several hundred meters away.

The Germans were very precise. Even in the horrible circumstances the captain wanted us to sign at the bottom of the page. But the whole thing collapsed because everyone on the list wasn't there. My father was away at a meeting of lighthouse keepers and my brother was at school. Also, when he interrogated my mother and me separately, we stuck to our stories.

In law school, I had studied enough of the armistice signed in 1940 by Marshal Pétain to know that German officials had to have proof that a person was in the Resistance in order to prosecute them. So I kept saying, "You've got to have evidence."

Even when they put us against the wall in the kitchen, I said again, "According to the terms of the armistice, you've got to have evidence."

I was the very essence of cool and, probably, foolhardiness. Outwardly, I knew no fear, although my mouth was dry and I had to fight to keep my voice steady.

When the captain stepped over to me, I noticed at once something that nearly caused me to faint. Those cold, green eyes, cleft chin, and chiseled features: I had seen them all before. This was the same officer who had so impatiently presided over the checkpoint in the Paris Metro the year before.

I had no real worry that he would remember me—an anonymous face in a crowd of nobodies he was herding around. But I did not want to show anything in my expression that raised any questions in his mind.

"A bit cheeky are we, mademoiselle?" he said, slightly amused at my effrontery.

My mother glanced at me nervously, imploring me with her eyes to keep quiet. I, on the other hand, knew my law and knew the German penchant for order. "Evidence, Herr Kapitan," I said sweetly, shrugging my shoulders and raising my hands palms up in a gesture of doggedness. The officer paused and stroked his perfect chin. He turned to the soldier who had accompanied them inside.

"Suche das haus," he shouted, gesturing toward the back and the trap door that led to the cellar. He motioned for my mother and me to sit down at the table. Her eyes were wild with fear, but I pleaded with my return glance that she not panic just yet.

One of the soldiers guarding the door joined the one inside, and they pulled up the door over the cellar and stepped carefully down the ladder. The officer sat across from us, watching with those horrible, all-seeing green eyes. I stared back at him as long as I could stand to do so, careful to keep my gaze somewhere between fear and hatred. He pulled a silver case out of the pocket of his tunic and pulled out a cigarette.

"Mind if I smoke, madame*?" he addressed my mother, as mistress of the house.*

She murmured her permission hesitantly, not looking directly at him. From below I could hear the soldiers searching the cellar, occasionally breaking jars. Every time I used the radio, I had returned it carefully to its hiding place in the well. The lid on the well was under some heavy barrels full of food. In a few more minutes, one of the soldiers shouted up to the captain.

"Nichts, Herr Kapitan."

The officer took a drag on his cigarette. "Genug."

The search was over. The men reappeared and one of them walked out the door.

"*Perhaps we were misinformed, ladies. Perhaps I owe you an apology.*"

"*Herr Kapitan,*" *the remaining soldier motioned for the officer to join him in the corner of the room. He began to whisper in his ear adamantly. At first I couldn't hear what he was saying, then I caught one word:* "*schieben.*"

The officer turned toward us. "*My trooper here wants to shoot you, even without any evidence of your wrongdoing.*" *He seemed to be considering what to do. The soldier started to speak, no doubt to press his case, but the officer held up his hand.* "Kommandant," *he said.*

The captain had decided to let the town commander determine our fate. That heartened me because I knew that the colonel in charge of the town was an army man first and not the diehard Nazi most men in his position usually were.

I relaxed, but then a new worry consumed me. I thought about all the guns stored in the attic, the guns my father had collected from all the wrecked planes. Our house was built in such a way that there were no inside stairs to the attic. We got there by climbing a ladder, which was always kept leaning against the back of the house.

I kept thinking, They'll see the ladder, find the guns, and then kill us. So far, however, the soldiers hadn't found anything, as they walked around outside the house.

About 11 A.M., only an hour after our ordeal had begun, the captain walked toward the door. He conferred with his men and turned toward us.

"*I'm afraid you will have to come with us to town,* madame," *he said to my mother.* "*We will need to question you further.*"

As I got up to accompany her, he motioned for me to stop. "*You will be staying here,* mademoiselle."

My mother seemed to be in a trance as she followed the tall officer outside. Tears streamed down my face as I watched her set out on foot. They were going to make her walk the twenty minutes it would take to get to town. The captain rode behind her in the van, his pistol drawn. The soldier who had made all the fuss was walking next to the vehicle with his machine gun pointing at her.

I was left alone, and it was then that I fell apart. My legs shook and I was a wreck. The sweat ran down my back and my face. I sat in a chair and steadied myself by rocking back and forth, my arms folded across my chest to hold myself together. After over an hour of this, I decided I needed to pull myself together. I thought about my Max and what he had given up. I thought of my mother in German custody. I simply had to take hold of myself.

Then a more practical concern occurred to me. I wondered about the ladder. I carried a basket as if I were going to cut lettuce in the garden and walked outside. I rounded the house and noticed immediately that the ladder wasn't where we usually kept it. I was both relieved and puzzled. Where was it? Then I remembered that it was the beginning of the cherry season, and my father had taken the ladder out in the fields. He hadn't brought it back.

My mother was released later that night and came home. As I had insisted, the Germans could find no evidence of illegal activity, despite what they had been told; although we were nervous for months that they would return, the German authorities never bothered us again.

Simone had ended her story at this point. In a note she explained that she intended to write more about what happened to her up

until the end of the war, about a year after the Germans interrogated her and her mother.

In spite of her earlier hopes, Allied forces landing in
Normandy headed east toward Paris and bypassed Brittany.
The Germans then moved forces west to reinforce the port cities against further invasions. The Germans dug in at the nearby
cities of Saint Nazaire and Lorient. Although isolated from the
main army, the troops in this region did not surrender until
May 8, 1945. The day before, the garrison in Le Croisic simply
disappeared. All of Simone's family survived, without further
problems.

"I want to tell the story of how the war made me a little
heroic before it dies with me," she wrote. "I was a witness to
an evil that must never be allowed to happen again. One way
to keep it from reappearing is to shed as much light as possible
on what happened to me and countless others. I think personal
stories like mine illuminate this terrible evil in a way history
books cannot. I am eager to show you more, Thomas, and discuss your ideas on how I might handle a few delicate subjects
not included here."

Monday

The next morning after breakfast, I reread Simone's story, this time with its salability in mind. I was moved by her quiet heroism and wanted to know more about what happened. But would a jaded, easily distracted reading public care? More importantly, would a jaded, easily distracted publisher be interested enough to give the public the chance to read it?

More than fifty-five years had passed since those events took place, and bookstores were inundated with books about the end of World War II and its aftermath. I wasn't sure Simone's writing would have a chance, but felt it was worth a try.

I puttered around all morning straightening up the house. I moved furniture, dusted, polished, and even washed windows. This close to the ocean, the salt spray creates a sludge-like film on the glass that makes it impossible to see out if left too long. This was probably going to be a weekly activity if I wanted to take advantage of the great view.

After lunch, I decided to call Simone and see if I could drive up for a chat about the book. More importantly: had she written more?

"Madame Godard's residence."

"Is this Rose?"

"Yes." The voice was wary.

"It's Tom Martindale. We met at the brunch yesterday."

"Yes." Still wary.

"Is Madame Godard there?"

"Just one moment."

As I waited, I idly thumbed through the manuscript on the table in front of me.

"Mr. Martindale? She is in the bath. She asks if you could come for drinks at six?"

"Tell her I'd love to, if she lets me take her out to dinner afterward."

"I'll let her know."

"Thanks, Rose. Will you also say I enjoyed what she gave me to read and am eager to see more?"

"And what might that have been?"

"She'll know."

"I'll pass along the message."

I drove to town to shop for groceries at the large Fred Meyer store. As I pushed my cart down the long aisles, I became aware of someone watching me. There he was: a tall, shabbily dressed man with wild hair and an unkempt beard. He was the kind of person I would usually cross the street to avoid. In this case, however, I had the odd feeling that I knew him.

"Hello, Martindale. Fancy meeting you here," he said, as I rolled into the wine section.

Yes, there was something vaguely familiar about his cold, dead-looking eyes.

"Gates? I didn't recognize you. How's it going?"

Charles Gates had worked at another Oregon university in marketing and public affairs until we had a run-in several years ago and he had been fired. Although I hadn't thought much about it at the time, I suppose he blamed me for his dismissal. Had I ruined his life so much that he looked like this? My cheery greeting hadn't gone over very well.

"Funny thing for you to ask, Martindale. I mean, you're the one who messed up my life."

He was standing with his face so close to mine I could smell the booze on his breath. Even though he was smiling and had not raised his voice, there was no mistaking the menace in his voice. Several people glanced over as they maneuvered their carts around us to get to the bottles of Paul Masson and Ernest and Julio Gallo.

I stepped back to gain some space and moved my shopping cart between us.

"Look, Gates, I'm not sure why you blame me for what happened to you. I'm not the one who made a fool of myself and acted crazy."

"Fool? Crazy?" He pushed the cart into me with a force that caused me to wince.

"Bad choice of words. Sorry." I remembered that a colleague had told me Gates had once undergone care in a psychiatric institution, a fact he had left off his resumé.

"You don't know what a big mistake you've just made by what you said."

I was in need of a change of subject. "So, what are you doing here? Having a little vacation on the coast?"

"Thanks to you, Martindale, I lost my job at the U of O. I've been reduced to selling ads for the Depoe Bay paper my uncle owns."

"Oh, I see. Well, at least you're still in advertising," I said cheerfully, suddenly becoming Mr. Every-Cloud-Has-a-Silver-Lining. Gates wasn't buying.

"You fucked me up good, Martindale, and I'll never forget it. Watch your back—I know that's what I'll be doing."

An odd look came over his face. He was smiling in a half-hearted way, but his eyes seemed not to be seeing me or anything else. He turned and walked away. I took a deep breath and felt someone looking at me.

"That man doesn't like you very much."

A youngish woman wearing a "Let's Have Fun on the Oregon Coast" sweatshirt was standing next to me, our shopping carts touching. Two kids with blank faces were standing in the cart, eyeing me intently.

"Well . . . er . . . an old landlord. He thinks I sold him out to the building inspectors." I had this ability to lie through my teeth at a moment's notice. I guess I picked it up during my years as an investigative reporter when I found it a useful skill. She didn't move. "Was there something else?"

She motioned toward the shelves behind me, as the little boy and girl stuck their tongues out. "I'm trying to get to that Ernest and Julio Gallo Chablis behind you. It's my husband's favorite."

"Oh, sure. Sorry."

I was surprised that the front door was open when I arrived at Simone's house shortly before six. I rang the bell and waited for a moment or so. I knocked on the door jamb. Nothing. I pushed the door open and stepped into the foyer.

"Simone. Hello?" I heard only the gentle ticking of a large clock and the distant rumbling of the sea against the cliffs.

I eased in a few more steps and stopped. It was several seconds before I became aware of loud sobbing. I entered the dining room, but it was empty. The sound was coming from the other side of the door, which was probably the kitchen.

I pushed in and found myself in a wonderful room, all tile and porcelain, with gleaming copper pots hanging from a circular rack above the cooking island in the center of the room. Rose Edwards was sitting at a small table by a window, head in her hands.

"Rose. What is it? What's happened?"

She looked up at me with eyes red and puffy from crying. "Who are you?"

"Tom Martindale. Simone's friend. We talked earlier. She invited me for drinks."

"Oh, yes. I remember."

"Where is Madame Godard, Rose?"

She seemed in shock, unable to think clearly. I walked to the sink and filled a glass with water.

"Drink this."

She didn't move.

"Something stronger? Liquor?"

She pointed to a cabinet near the dining room door. I selected cognac, filled a glass I found in the cabinet, and offered it to Rose.

"Drink this. It'll make you feel better."

She emptied the glass quickly, and I poured another shot.

"Are you feeling better?"

She nodded, as I pulled out a chair and sat next to her.

"Why are you so upset? Did something happen to Madame Godard?"

"She went to help my son, Adam."

I remembered Simone mentioning him the night before, something about him being retarded and how she sometimes helped him out of scrapes. He was the guy I had seen at the lighthouse.

"Yes, Simone told me she has helped him before. You called to her as I was leaving and said he was in some trouble. I remember that. What trouble and what was she trying to do?"

Rose avoided my eyes, perhaps trying to decide if she could trust me.

"Rose, I can't help you or Madame Godard or your son if you won't tell me what this is about."

"You'll help Adam?"

She was sounding unfocused. I took her hands and looked directly into her face.

"Yes, Rose. I'll help Adam if I can. Now tell me what happened."

"He works for an undertaker, digging graves and helping out. You know my Adam's not right. I had him late in life. My husband and I'd given up having any kids, but we kept trying. I'd had a lot of miscarriages so I was pleased as punch when I found out I was pregnant. I took real good care of myself, but it wasn't good enough. He looked normal, but he didn't act right. He couldn't learn much, and the doctors said he'd never develop up here . . ."—she pointed to her head—" . . . more than maybe an eight year old. I guess I didn't have what it takes to nourish him properly. It like to nearly killed my husband. He wanted a son to teach how to hunt and fish. Adam couldn't do neither one. He was ashamed of him, and he wouldn't talk to him. He started drinking heavily, and one day he just keeled over at work."

She stared off into space.

"I've tried to do my best with Adam. He's really a sweet boy, now a man, I suppose. Madame Godard has helped a lot since I came to work here over two years ago. She even got Adam his job."

"She's wonderful that way, I know. Tell me what happened today."

"The undertaker accused him of stealing some money, and madame said she'd talk to him."

"You mean Adam denied it?"

"Oh, yes. He wouldn't steal money. He doesn't know what money is, really. He gives what he earns to me, and I put it in the bank. I'm saving up for the day when I won't be here to help him."

"You've set up some kind of trust fund?"

"Yes. That nice Mr. Andrews, madame's lawyer, helped me. She was going to contribute, although I don't think Mr. Andrews thought she should. . . . But anyway, Adam was hysterical and kept insisting that Madame Godard go with him to the Yaquina Head Lighthouse to meet his boss."

"The lighthouse? That seems pretty odd, I mean for a meeting spot. Why there?"

"Adam's always liked to go there since he was a little boy. He loves all the gulls flying around and the flashing of the light as it swirls around. I guess both Adam's boss and Madame Godard decided that a meeting there would calm him down. She loves lighthouses herself. You know she grew up in one in France. Her father was a lighthouse keeper."

"Yes, she told me."

"So, she didn't think twice about going down there when he suggested it, and off they went about 3:30. She said she'd be back in time to meet you. I just have this terrible feeling that something bad has happened to her and my Adam. I was desperate to help him, but then I got worried that I'd gotten her into something bad."

She started crying again, and I got up to put my hand on her shoulder.

"I'm sure there's some logical reason. I'll go down and see if I can find them. We'll all be back in no time."

Summer traffic on Highway 101 is terrible, even on the best days. I hadn't driven very far before I realized that things were moving even slower than usual. The line of cars, campers, RVs, and all kinds of trucks turned sluggish at the top of Cape Foulweather. It got worse as two lanes merged into one south of the high promontory. Just before we got to the turnoff to Beverly Beach State Park, traffic stopped altogether.

Up ahead I could see the flashing lights of police cars. After five minutes of sitting with our motors idling, many drivers turned off their ignitions and got out to stretch and talk to one another. Soon, I joined them.

"Must be an accident."

"Probably."

"Didn't hear an ambulance."

"It'd come from the south, from Newport. Maybe we couldn't hear the siren from here."

"Oh, Herb, of course you'd hear the siren. Sirens are loud."

And so on.

After ten minutes or so, a state police officer came driving slowly toward us from the south. He was informing people about the delay as he went by.

"Bad accident up ahead . . . be here some time."

I could only hear snatches of what he was saying. Finally, he pulled up to where I was standing.

"How long?" I asked before he could speak.

"One hour, maybe two. There's been a fatality."

"Man or woman?"

"Young boy, actually. Somehow fell out of the back of a pickup and hit his head. Looks like he didn't have a chance."

"Only a kid. What a shame. Why will it take so long?"

"Body fell across the center line so it's straddling the highway in both directions. We've got to wait for the coroner before we can move the body. He's down in Waldport, so it's taking a while."

He drove on to repeat the same litany to the drivers behind me.

I got back into my car to figure out what to do. The delay made me uneasy because I felt the need to find Simone as soon as possible. I could see the blinking beam of the lighthouse, a half-mile or so to the southwest. It was nearly eight and would be dark in another half-hour to forty-five minutes. I was beginning to get a nervous feeling in my stomach as I thought about Simone Godard and what might have happened to her. I couldn't wait any longer.

I turned the key. With care, I could ease my car around to the left onto the shoulder, then glide next to the two cars in front of me and into the parking area located ahead. I made the maneuver with plenty of room to spare. No one seemed surprised that I was leaving the highway.

After pulling my car into the last parking space in the lot, I got out, looked up and down the shoreline, and began walking slowly down an incline. I strolled nonchalantly down the beach toward the lighthouse, its glimmering light beckoning. Luckily, the tide was going out so I was able to walk without any trouble. And by staying on the wet sand, which was firmly packed, I made remarkably good time.

It was a pleasant evening, and I was glad for the chance to walk along one of the nicest beaches in Oregon. Even though I had access to a beach near my house, I tended to think I was too busy. I vowed to take time in the future; being so close to the ocean always helped clear my head and cleanse my soul.

I reached the cliffs below the lighthouse in a half-hour, then kept going south until I reached a flat area containing tide pools. These wonderful indentations in the rocks are where each new tide deposits all kinds of sea creatures, which dwell in the crevices for a time before being washed out to sea again. It was interesting to prowl around these pools, but I had no time tonight. Instead, I walked up the gradual slope and reached the road at about 8:45. I looked down the road to my right toward the rock quarry, which shared the Yaquina Head with the lighthouse.

The lights were out in the visitors' center straight ahead of me, and the gates had been closed and locked. I hoped I wouldn't encounter a stray tourist or Bureau of Land Management staff member, but didn't as I hurried left around the curve toward the lighthouse.

Suddenly, I thought I saw movement in the brush near the building. I had to rely on random flashes from the beacon above and the fading twilight to see anything.

"Is someone there?"

The roar of the sea and the mournful cawing of distant seabirds was all I heard in reply. I made my way up the path to the lighthouse, wondering how I would get inside. If Adam and Simone were still there, as unlikely as that seemed, they would probably be inside. I turned the knob on the ancient door, and it opened easily, hinges creaking loudly. I entered the lower room.

The building was old: 1872 was chiseled into a panel above the front door. I guess it had earned its moldy smell. From the beacon's light reflecting off the walls, I could just make out the dim outline of a spiral staircase in another room at the end of a short hall. I walked slowly, half afraid to go up, but knowing I could do nothing else.

"Simone? Adam?" My words echoed in the tall tower. I counted one hundred fourteen steps to the top—a total height of ninety-three feet, I had read in a guidebook somewhere. I paced myself, but was out of breath when I reached the top.

The stairs ended in a small room at the top of the lighthouse. Above me, the electronic beacon pulsated—two seconds on, two seconds off. Unlike the candle or coal oil lights of old, which had to be tended round the clock, this one was automatic.

I climbed a small ladder to reach the actual top, with large-paned windows comprising the dome. Most were immovable, but I soon found one that opened, its hinges squeaking as I swung it aside to go down.

I rested for a moment to marvel at the spectacle: gulls circling over my head in and out of visibility, the long sweep of the lighthouse's stone walls, which vanished in the starry night well above the sea below, the roar of the surf, and the taste of salt air on my lips.

As I turned to walk away, something caught my eye. I climbed out onto the narrow platform, feeling very vulnerable and not daring to look down. I groped my way to a large object, only to catch my foot on something metallic, which clattered loudly as I fell over it. My face hit the grating so hard I was sure its serpentine pattern had made an imprint on my face.

I got to my knees and picked up the object—a garden spade. As I focused on the tool, the beacon above me skittered around long enough for me to see both the blood on its blunt end and the battered head of Simone Godard only a few inches from where I had fallen.

5

I felt sick to my stomach, but controlled the impulse. There wasn't time or space on this narrow platform. If I wasn't careful, I'd be joining Simone, except my death would be from an accidental plunge into the ocean.

I maneuvered myself into a sitting position and carefully put the spade down. I had touched the handle, but not the end with the blood on it. There was just too much at stake for me to let myself be found here, my fingerprints on a murder weapon. An investigation of me—and possibly my arrest—would only distract the police from what they should be doing: finding Simone's killer. At the same time, I was aware of what an arrest would do to my career, even if I quickly cleared my name. All that I had worked toward for over twenty years could be jeopardized by casually picking up a garden tool. I simply couldn't let that happen.

Taking a handkerchief out of my pocket, I carefully wiped the handle, making sure not to touch the blood on the blunt end. I then put it back where I had first stumbled on it. I looked at Simone one last time before going back inside. My eyes filled with tears as I thought of this wonderful person who had gone through so much in her life.

I made my descent rapidly, glad for the darkness. I wanted to retrace my steps out through the tide pools, but didn't feel sure enough to try to follow that route in the dark. I decided to go back another way.

Heading east, I skirted the top of the steep cliffs above a cove and then climbed up a hill in the general direction of where my car was. I was winded by the time I reached the line of shore pines whose tops had been gnarled by the wind. They formed the boundary of the Head. I was tired, but I didn't stop. I turned to my left and walked along the fence, hoping to find a break in it.

"Hey, watch what you're doing."

I froze.

"Oh, come on, Janny. You promised we'd do it this time."

I peered through an opening in the trees. Two kids, probably no more than sixteen or seventeen, were lying on a blanket only a few feet away. I spotted a parking lot beyond.

"I never did any such thing, Jared. I'm a nice girl."

"Why'd you even agree to this date, then? What'd you think we'd do up here—look at the lighthouse?"

My sentiments exactly, I thought to myself.

I crept along as quietly as I could and decided first that my prurient thoughts were best kept unaroused, and second, that these two wouldn't be able to get a good look at me on the other side of the fence. But I stepped on a dry branch.

"What was that, Jared?"

Janny was now lying on the blanket, her earlier resistance apparently set aside; Jared, in the process of unbuttoning his jeans, seemed not to notice the sound.

"I didn't hear nothing."

"Anything."

"What?"

"I said, anything. The proper word to use in that sentence is anything, not nothing."

I kept walking.

"Jared. Why are you putting your pants back on?"

"Shit, Janny. I just hate it when you correct my grammar. It makes me feel real stupid."

Pretending to be an evening jogger, I made it to my car in thirty minutes and saw that the accident had been cleared away. Although Highway 101 had fewer hindrances than the beach, I kept having to avoid oncoming traffic; at one point, an older model Honda slowed down across the road, then sped away.

It was around ten when I unlocked my car door and quickly slipped on a sweatshirt and changed into tennis shoes so I would look more casual. I had formed a plan, and it was time to act on it.

I then drove the distance down to the Yaquina Head turnoff in ten minutes and turned toward the main gate on a side road. This time, I intended to make my presence known.

As I expected, the usual barrier had been set up at dusk so no car could get down the hill to the tide pools and lighthouse. I got out of the car and picked up the receiver on the emergency phone attached to a small wooden box on the side of the road.

"BLM emergency center. How may I help you?"

"I'm at the gate to the Yaquina Head Lighthouse. I'm looking for a friend I was supposed to meet. I think she's probably on the grounds, but it's so dark, I don't think I can find her. Then I saw the gate and the phone. So I called."

"Your name please, sir?"

"Tom Martindale."

"Spell that for me, please."

"M-A-R-T-I-N-D-A-L-E."

"And your friend's name?"

"Simone Godard." I spelled both names before being asked to do so.

"Any reason to suspect foul play?"

"No. I was supposed to meet her hours ago, but I got hung up in a traffic accident on 101, and when I got here—like I already said, she isn't around."

"Please stay where you are, and I'll send someone."

"Should I start looking?" I asked, wanting the answer I expected to be in the official record.

"No, sir. It's much too dark. Just wait in your car. You are in a car, aren't you?"

"Yes. I'll just sit tight."

I spent the half-hour it took for help to arrive contemplating my next move. I knew I would try to find Simone's killer, no matter how long it took. What had caused her death? Something in her manuscript? Someone from her past? Adam Edwards? He would probably be a suspect because she had been on her way to meet him. But was he capable of such violence? From what his mother had told me, I doubted it.

My thoughts were interrupted by headlights from a pickup truck coming up behind me. A tall man wearing the brown uniform of a Bureau of Land Management employee got out of the vehicle and headed toward me. He was carrying a flashlight.

"Mr."—he consulted a paper in his hand—"Martin? . . ."

Why did such an easy name always make people react like it was Polish or Thai?

" . . . dale. Call me Tom. Hi, thanks for coming."

"George Hastings."

We shook hands.

"So, your friend is missing, and you think she's in here on the grounds somewhere?"

"Yeah. Her name is Simone Godard. She's a lady of seventy-five or so, and I'm worried that she's injured and in need of help."

"Of course, sir. We'll drive on in and take a look." He unlocked and opened the gate. I followed him back to the truck and got in the passenger side. He turned on the ignition, and we headed down the hill toward the lighthouse.

I couldn't lead my new friend right to Simone's body, of course. I would have to let this play out, no matter how long it took or how guilty I felt for prolonging her stay on the platform above.

"Here we are," Hastings said, as he stopped the truck in front of the lighthouse building. He glanced over and frowned. "That's funny. Looks like the door to the lighthouse is wide open. The guide's supposed to lock up after the last tourist leaves."

He picked up his flashlight and motioned toward the glove compartment. "There's another one of these in there." I retrieved its twin and we got out.

"Where do we look first?" I wanted to appear as uncertain as possible.

"Why don't you walk around the building along that path on the left and up on the deck. Don't worry, it's safe. There are guardrails when you reach the back. I'm going to have a look at the building and see if I can figure out why that door was left open."

As directed, I walked down the narrow path through thick salal trampled by thousands of tourist feet over the years. I could hear but not see the ocean, and its salt spray was soon on my face, leaving a bitter taste in my mouth. I beamed my light around languidly, waiting for the shout I expected any minute.

"Tom. Tom! Are you down there?"

He had found Simone's body.

I ran around the building and in through the open door. I made the ascent a lot faster this time, because I knew the way. When I got to the top, I walked to the open window and stuck my head out. George Hastings was kneeling, the spade in his hand.

"I didn't find your friend, but I found this."

Tuesday

I woke up the next morning feeling sad. It had taken me a long time to get to sleep the night before. I had tossed and turned for over an hour as I ran the events of the evening over and over in my mind. Simone Godard was dead. I had no doubt about that. But who had killed her and then moved her body? Those were the questions I knew I had to answer.

So far, I had kept myself out of things so that distance would give me room to maneuver.

The night before, I had managed to escape notice because George Hastings, the BLM guy, had taken charge and told me to go home. He, after all, was the one who found the bloody spade. It was too dark to do much searching, so we agreed to keep in touch. He said he would look for Simone this morning and notify the police. I was too exhausted and dispirited to argue.

My instinct had told me to insist on a search right then, with klieg lights and helicopters. But I knew there would be no chance to find Simone alive, so I elected to follow his lead, a better stance to provide me deniability later. I intended to call Hastings and drive back to the lighthouse as soon as I got dressed. I also needed to call Rose Edwards and tell her what I had found out.

I sat on the edge of the bed and stretched, then got up, stripped off my shorts and walked into the bathroom for a soothing shower. I never sang or talked to myself during this morning ritual, so I was shocked to hear voices from the front of the house as I was toweling off and stepping out onto the tile floor. Had a radio somehow been turned on? Or my TV?

"There's the good professor. Step on out here so we can see you."

I jumped so hard the towel I had wrapped around my waist nearly fell down. "What the hell?"

As the steam in the bathroom evaporated, I made out the dumpy figure of someone I had hoped I would never meet again: Art Kutler, the local sheriff. Ten years before, when he was younger and thinner but no less slovenly, Kutler had suspected my involvement in another murder and had done everything possible to hinder my efforts to help my friend who was charged clear her name. We had a number of arguments over that.

I had revealed his part in blowing up a whale carcass on the beach near my house. After film footage that showed him being showered with whale parts was replayed repeatedly on television, he had become a laughingstock in the community. As a result, he was not reelected. Even though he eventually lived that down to the extent that he won another term several years later, I doubt he remembered me with any fondness.

"Hello, sheriff. I don't suppose you'd have anything resembling a search warrant to show for breaking into my house?"

Under the circumstances, I should have been scared about seeing him again. In fact, I had been dreading it since returning to the coast. But Kutler was such a predictable idiot that he always brought out the wisecracking, tough guy in me, no matter how risky.

"Didn't need it. The door was unlocked, and I was concerned for your welfare."

"Yeah, sure, sheriff. What do you want?"

"First of all, maybe you'd like to get dressed. We're going for a little ride, you and me. That is, unless you'd like to parade around naked in front of the world. By the way, doctor, you don't look too bad without your clothes on. How's come a nice-looking guy like you isn't married?"

I ignored his goading and, for effect, made a big deal out of dropping the towel and walking over to my bureau. Normally, I'm the most modest of people, but Kutler had made me so mad I exhibited just the opposite.

"Do you mind, sheriff?"

He shrugged his shoulders and turned around, pausing to stand with his back to me in the doorway. I quickly put on shorts, socks, chinos, and a yellow polo shirt, and sat on the bed to lace up my sneakers. I then walked back into the bathroom to comb my hair and brush my teeth. Shaving would have to wait.

"Okay, sheriff. Let's sit out in the living room so you can tell me why you have unlawfully invaded my privacy."

Kutler, a man with no sense of the absurd, did not appreciate the sarcasm.

"I could haul your ass to jail for fleeing the scene of a crime, professor. Your old friend Angela Pride isn't here to help you get out of this like last time."

For some reason, Kutler had always resented my being a college professor. His conversations were always heavy with snotty asides about people who waste taxpayers' money by not working very hard. Every time he addressed me, it was always by a formal title, pronounced with an edge. I ignored his reference to Angela, a close friend who was with the Oregon State Police.

I motioned for him to sit while I headed into the kitchen to make coffee. I didn't want to be hospitable, but I needed something to jump-start my system. Also, I knew it would make him mad. He didn't sit down, but walked to the front door and huddled with two deputies just outside.

"I want to talk to you now," he said, as he came back in.

"Relax, sheriff. Sit down here, and we'll talk like rational human beings." I smiled, as I placed two cups on the bar.

"Don't patronize me, Martindale."

"I wouldn't think of it, sheriff. Now what's this about fleeing the scene of a crime?" I smiled again, even less sincerely than before.

"I'm asking the questions here."

We both fell silent and watched the coffee maker run through its cycle. I filled both cups.

"Cream or sugar?"

He shook his head while I sat down across from him.

"Okay, now what is this all about?"

He took a big gulp, then gasped as the coffee burned his throat, spilling the brew on his shirt. He madly wiped his mouth and started brushing coffee off his clothing.

"Careful. It might be hot," I said belatedly. I got up, tore off a paper towel, and handed it to him. "Here. For your uniform."

"Hotter than it looked."

He was still dabbing at his uniform, when he said, "Why I'm here, yes. Do you know a Frenchwoman by the name of . . ." He started fumbling in his shirt pocket, first for glasses, then for a slip of paper. He opened the glasses case and put on half-glasses that looked incongruous on his large, round face. "See-moan Goe-dart."

"Yes, sheriff. I know her well." In my few encounters with police in the past, I learned not to blurt out information that goes beyond what is asked. My normal chatty style would be misplaced.

"Her housekeeper reported her missing and said you'd gone looking for her yesterday."

"That's right, sheriff. She and I were supposed to have dinner. When I got to her house, Mrs. Edwards said she'd headed to Newport, so I drove down here to find her and take her out to dinner." I paused, trying to gauge how Kutler was taking all of this. He was daring another sip of coffee, blowing on it first.

"And?"

"I was driving to the Yaquina Head Lighthouse—that's where Rose Edwards said she'd gone—but got delayed by a traffic accident a mile or so north. I guess somebody got killed?"

He nodded and kept sipping.

"Anyway, by the time I got to the gates of the Head, they were locked. I was concerned about Madame Godard, so I used the emergency phone and called the BLM emergency center. It was completely dark by then, and I didn't want to go crashing around the Head. After all, sheriff, the gate was locked."

He paused to consider what I was saying. He no doubt knew what had happened next, but was probably wondering what I'd say, hoping I'd contradict what George Hastings had reported. I felt fairly safe in continuing.

"I waited by the gate for someone from the BLM to arrive. A guy named Hastings showed up, and we went inside and started searching. While I looked around outside the lighthouse, he went inside. Pretty soon he called down to me. I climbed up and he showed me a garden spade with blood on it. He said he'd call the police. We agreed it was too dark to do much more, so I came home. Got here about midnight and went to bed."

"You never saw hide nor hair of this Frenchwoman?"

"No. No sign at all."

"Why didn't you report her being missing?"

"I didn't know she was missing. I followed Hastings's lead. He said he'd call the police."

Kutler pulled out several folded pages from his pocket and read them. I drank my coffee and waited for him to speak. "That pretty much squares with what Hastings told us. Mrs. Edwards mentioned the mortician, Chapman. We checked, and he has an alibi." Kutler was predictable. He was always trying to trip me up. I'd forget about his unlawful entry into my house. Being cool was the best stance to take now.

Kutler got up and took off his glasses. "That about does it, doctor. I'll call you if I need any more. You're going to be around for the summer?"

"Yeah, I'll be here. May I ask about the search for Madame Godard?"

"Oh, didn't I say?" He was really smirking now. "A fisherman found her body a few miles north of here earlier today. We've put out an APB for Mrs. Edwards's son Adam. I think he's our killer."

Before I could say anything, Sheriff Kutler bolted from the room, the self-satisfied smile still on his face.

Kutler's revelation left me with a hundred questions, but I knew the sheriff wouldn't tell me much more than he already had. I would have gotten angrier—and he haughtier—if I had tried to find out more about the facts. His real aim had been to toy with me and make me squirm, and he had accomplished that.

The sheriff's information also left me with a knot in my stomach. Simone Godard was someone I had liked and admired a great deal. This vital, intelligent woman would have hated such an inelegant death—alone on a desolate headland. Alone, that is, with her killer.

I picked up my cell phone, looked up a number, and dialed.

"Angela Pride, this is your old pal Tom Martindale." I was using my best radio voice to leave a message on the voice mail of an old friend, the Oregon State Police officer in charge of security at the university. "Please call me at home in Newport. I need to ask you a question."

I pushed the disconnect button and punched in another number.

"Hello, Rose. It's Tom Martindale."

Simone's housekeeper sounded hoarse. "Yes, Mr. Martindale. I was going to call you. I feel so bad about Madame Godard. And I'm worried about my Adam." Her voice broke, and she started sobbing.

"Rose. Listen to me. Calm down. I'm coming over. Rose, can you hear me?"

"Yes. I have something to show you."

"I'm on my way."

I hung up the phone and looked around to make sure everything in the house was secure—stove off, doors and windows locked. For safety's sake, I took Simone's manuscript and locked it in the trunk of my car, making a mental note to remember to bring it back inside later.

It took twenty minutes to get to the Godard house in Depoe Bay. It felt eerie to be doing the same things I had done two days before when it had been a very pleasant occasion. I parked in the turnaround and walked up to the door. Rose Edwards opened the door before I knocked.

"Come in, Mr. Martindale."

I stepped into the foyer, and she motioned for me to follow her into the living room. She continued toward a room I had only glimpsed before, the room I assumed was Simone's study.

She opened the door and stepped aside to allow me to enter. What had once been a tiny refuge of elegant order was now totally trashed. Books from the floor-to-ceiling shelves on three walls were dumped into heaps on the floor; chairs and a sofa were overturned, their cushions slashed; the contents of a filing cabinet were strewn around, as were all the things that had been on her desk. It would have been a disgusting and horrifying sight under any circumstances. But coming so soon after Simone's death, it was sickening.

As I made my way through the debris, my eyes were drawn to her computer. There on the flickering screen was a Nazi swastika.

I sat down to examine this emblem of evil more closely. It was the home page of one of those hate groups.

Rose Edwards was still standing in the doorway. I turned to face her.

"When did you find all this?"

"This morning just before you called. I'd been keeping to the back of the house since last night when I locked up. My room is next to the kitchen, way at the other end of the house. On my way to get the paper, I saw that the door was open. I thought I had closed it last night. Then I saw the mess."

"And you hadn't heard anything?"

She shook her head. "I took a sleeping pill after I decided madame wasn't coming back. Adam said . . ." She paused, as if she had second thoughts.

I switched off the computer and got up. "Why don't we sit down in the living room?" I took her by the arm with one hand and gently closed the study door, as if to close out one unpleasantness while dealing with another. Rose sighed heavily.

"I want to help you, and I want to help Adam, Rose." I was tried to sound as reassuring as I could.

She was looking directly up at me, tears forming. "I know," she said, dabbing her eyes with a tissue.

"You saw Adam last night after I was here?"

"Yes." She cleared her throat and squared her shoulders. "He knocked on my window after midnight, and I let him in the back door."

"Did he tell you what happened?"

"He says he waited for Madame Godard for a while, then decided she wasn't coming, so he left and went to what he calls his special place at the lighthouse."

"Special place?"

She hesitated, and I knew she was holding something back. "I'm . . . not . . . sure. I just know he likes the lighthouse and spends a lot of time there when he's not working."

"You mean he sleeps there?"

"No, not in the lighthouse. The cemetery owner lets him sleep in a small building on the grounds. He's here sometimes, and I feed him—with madame's permission, of course."

"That's a long way from the lighthouse. What about what you said earlier—about a special place?" I was feeling impatient.

"That's all I know."

"All right. Let's forget about that. What did he say happened next?"

She sighed and seemed relieved. "He waited for a while— I can't be sure how long. Adam doesn't relate to time in the same way we do. He can tell time, but doesn't have a watch or anything. He goes by a kind of intuition. If he's hungry when the light is strongest, it must be noon. If it gets dark and he feels sleepy, it's time to go to bed. I know it sounds odd, but it works for Adam."

"You were saying what he did then."

"Oh, yes, sorry. He said he went back to the lighthouse. The door was open, so he walked up the stairs. I think I told you he's always been fascinated with it. He likes the way the beacon goes around and shines . . ." She was searching for a word, using one finger to trace a circle in the air.

" . . . haphazardly?"

"Yes, that's it, haphazardly, on one side and then the other. He says the light is chasing him."

"So he climbed to the top, and what happened?"

"He was looking out to sea, and he noticed something on the platform outside."

"Did he say what?"

"He called it a monster, and he got scared and ran down the steps."

"What do you think the monster was?"

"I assume it was Madame Godard's body."

"Why do you say that? The sheriff told me her body was found a few miles north of the lighthouse."

"I just assumed, I mean from what Adam said."

"You're sure he didn't go out onto the platform and take a look?"

"I don't think so. I know Adam and how much he fears the unknown. Mentally handicapped people function best when they're kept in a routine. When Adam does the same thing day in and day out and takes his meds, he doesn't get agitated or unhappy."

"Did he see the bloody spade?"

I instantly bit my lip.

"The police didn't say anything about that."

I tried to camouflage my faux pas.

"Yes, apparently. The murder weapon was a spade."

"Oh, my God," she gasped and stood up. "Adam uses something like that in his work at the cemetery, I think. You know, he digs graves and maintains the grounds to earn money."

I nodded.

"They'll hunt him down. He won't know what to do. He's like a child." She slumped back down in her chair.

"Rose, why don't you fix us some tea? I think that will make us both feel better. We can collect our thoughts and figure out what to do."

"You'll help Adam and me?"

I nodded, wondering what I was getting into. I then led her into the kitchen. We had our tea in silence until she put some scones on a plate and placed them and a jar of jam on the table in front of me.

"Can you tell me anything about Madame Godard's last hours here before she left?" I asked.

"Nothing unusual happened yesterday that I saw," she said.

"She told me she thought someone might be trying to kill her. Do you know anything about that?"

"She swore me to secrecy, but . . ."

"I have to know everything if I'm going to help you and Adam."

"Yes, of course," she replied. "This secret isn't going to do her any good now, I suppose."

She paused for a moment.

"Several days ago, maybe two days before you came for brunch, Madame Godard told me that a car had tried to pass her on Cape Foulweather and cut her off. It was where the road narrows as you start descending, and I guess this large van with darkened windows went flying by her on the right, then seemed to slow down so fast she almost ran into it. She managed to pass him and get away. She has . . . had . . . a big

Lincoln and didn't mind driving it fast."

"Was it day or night?"

"About midnight, I think. She had been at the symphony in Newport."

"She didn't say anything about a license number?"

"I remember she said the van didn't have any license plates. I mean, it was like a ghost car." She shuddered slightly.

"Did the van follow her home?"

"I gather she lost him and turned off 101 before he could see where she was going. She was fast for an old lady." She smiled as she visualized the scene, then looked over her shoulder as if she expected Simone to come through the door and reprimand her for being so frank.

"What about burial plans and her will?"

"Her attorney Verne Andrews is handling that. He called me this morning and said he'd be by to talk to me this afternoon. I'm sure I'll have to move out when this house is sold."

"One other thing. Madame Godard mentioned to me that she didn't like Fred Bader very much—her colleague from the department?"

"She didn't say anything about that to me. He was here last night."

"When?"

"About an hour after you left to meet her. I told him what I told you—about Adam and the lighthouse. I guess I shouldn't have blabbed all of that, but I'd met him a number of times over the years and felt he was a friend. When I told him where she was, he started talking to the other gentleman who was here with him."

"Another man?"

"Yes, another German man, I think. I couldn't tell what they were saying because they spoke German. He said he needed to pick up some papers from her and asked if he could go into the study."

"And did he?"

"Oh, no, I couldn't permit that, not when madame wasn't home. I lied and told him the door was locked, and that she had the only key."

"This other man. What did he look like?"

"A bit like Mr. Bader—I mean fine features and fair complexion, hair parted in the middle. He was pretty polite."

"Did you get his name?"

"Mr. Bader introduced me, but the name escapes me now—some complicated German name. I'm afraid I have enough trouble with English and madame's French without understanding anything like German."

We both stared at the table for a few moments. She broke the silence.

"There was one other thing about him I just remembered. He had these beautiful green eyes. I mean they locked into you, and you couldn't look away. I was like in a trance or something. They were like . . . what are those things that can shoot through walls?"

"You mean lasers?"

"Yes, that's it. His green eyes were like lasers."

W hen I got home later that morning, I had a message from Angela Pride. I called her back right away.

"Angela Pride, Oregon State Police."

"Tom Martindale, professor and journalist extraordinaire."

"Tom. I thought I was going to be rid of you for a while, have the summer to catch up on my other work with you safely off campus."

Even if Angela hadn't always been satisfied with our earlier relationship, she had gotten something from it: a sense of humor. She seldom revealed it to anyone else, however. To the rest of the world, she was just the stiff-necked, wrinkle-free police automaton she had been when I met her. With me, she loosened up and laughed at the ridiculousness of life. I was glad we had gotten beyond the pain and awkwardness of our breakup.

"You sound bored, Angela. I can see you sitting there in your neatly pressed OSP uniform, picking lint off one sleeve as you clean your gun. The sexiest looking OSP officer in the state, the only OSP officer in the state who irons her bras."

"That I will ignore. And I'll bet you are sitting wherever you are dressed in pants, shirt, and a tie with seagull crap on it."

I was known for my collection of ties with varying motifs and degrees of garishness.

"Actually, I'm not wearing many ties this summer, especially that seagull one. I had to throw it away, it got so smelly."

"Enough of this, Tom," she laughed. "I know you well enough to suspect an ulterior motive. What mess are you into now?"

"I'm hurt that I'm that transparent. Yeah, you're right. I'm a little worried about getting into trouble over here."

"God, Tom. You're not putting on your private eye hat again? Since I've known you, you've been hit on the head, chased by bad guys, thrown over several cliffs—you name it. And that was before you got tenure."

She was making fun of me and loving it. I was enjoying this banter too, primarily because it meant we were still good friends.

"Okay, Angela. I admit I get too involved when a friend is in trouble."

"What is it this time?"

"It's your old pal, Sheriff Kutler."

"I thought he'd retired."

"No, he's still very much on duty. I woke up this morning with him practically joining me in the shower."

"Sounds pretty kinky for Art. Sure you're thinking of the right guy?"

"Oh, yeah, it was him all right."

I gave Angela the rundown on what Kutler had told me and what had taken place at the lighthouse. I told her about Adam Edwards, but I didn't mention the fact that I had found Simone's body before someone moved it. I decided to hold onto that bit of information until it seemed safe to reveal it.

"So, Art didn't seem to suspect you?"

"No, I think he was just trying to rattle my cage like always. Isn't it a bit unusual for the sheriff himself to make a routine call to my house?"

"Yes, very. He always seems to let you get under his skin. You can be very irritating, Tom," she laughed.

"Thanks, Angela."

"Not to those of us who know you," she added quickly, still laughing.

"Okay. I know I can be pushy. I'm just telling you all this so you'll know what happened."

"You're not going to do one of your investigations, are you? You need to stick to writing and leave the detective work to me and my colleagues."

"I did tell . . ." I was mumbling.

"Speak up, Tom. Something wrong with the connection?"

"I told Adam's mother, Rose, that I'd try to help her. I'd just like to make sure the legal system doesn't make mincemeat of him. He's retarded, Angela. He won't know what's happening to him if he's arrested."

"I see your point. Let me do this much: I'll look into it, even though it's way out of my jurisdiction. For now, let me give you the name of the trooper in charge of the Newport office. He's got my old job. His name is Nate Golden. You'll like him. He's a young guy and has a sense of humor. He's a New Yorker, I think, or from one of those states back east. Anyway, he talks kind of funny. I'll call around and test the waters with Nate and Kutler. I'll get back to you."

"Thanks, Angela. I appreciate it."

"And Tom?"

"Yes."

"Don't make me sorry I helped you. Don't get into a mess. Do you promise?"

"Of course not, Angela. I learned my lesson the last time."

"I hope so, Tom, I really do."

Angela Pride knew me better than I imagined, I thought to myself when I hung up the phone. I wanted to avoid another involvement with a murder, of course, but how could I walk away from a friend like Simone? I didn't think Adam Edwards was capable of killing anyone, but I knew the sheriff had already stopped looking for any other suspects. I had to locate him first.

If not Adam, who else had something to gain from Simone's death? Had her killer been one of the guests at brunch? Their faces came to mind: Verne Andrews, her attorney; Connie Wright, the voracious divorcée; Stacy Thomas, her former student, and her jealous boyfriend, Joe George; and Manfred Bader, her German colleague, and his mousy wife, Elaine. They all seemed benign enough at the time.

I brewed some coffee and sat drinking it at the desk in my study, looking out at the trees and rocky cliffs and the sea beyond. Then my eyes settled on Simone's manuscript. All the events in her story took place so long ago that there seemed scant connection to today. And it had all taken place in France, about as far removed from the coast of Oregon as you could possibly be. But Simone had hinted at a connection. I had to find it.

On a whim, I decided to begin my search for Adam Edwards by talking to his boss at the mortuary. Rose Edwards had said it adjoined a cemetery and was south of the Yaquina Bay Bridge at the other end of town. Maybe I would also discover where he hung out at the lighthouse.

The telephone directory listed only one such establishment: Sea View Mortuary and Cemetery, Lyle Chapman, proprietor. I dialed the number and a woman answered after one ring.

"Sea View Mortuary. Nadine speaking."

"Yes, hello. My name is Martin, and I wondered if I could come in and talk to you about burying my aunt. I hear you have very good facilities. Could I have a tour?"

"Of course, Mr. Martin. We are open until five."

"I'll see you in a half-hour, then."

Sea View Mortuary was in a beautiful setting. The grounds were professionally maintained with thick, green turf and a row of colorful flowers on either side of the long driveway. On closer inspection, I could see that the lawn stretched up the hill to the south and extended into the adjoining cemetery.

The mortuary itself was in a building that looked very out of place on the Oregon coast: a Spanish hacienda complete with courtyard and splashing fountain. I parked my car next to a big Lincoln Town Car with the dealer's paper sticker still on the window.

The smell of formaldehyde and pine disinfectant burned my nostrils as I stepped into a large entry hall. A large woman wearing silk pajamas came through the doorway on my right. She was smiling and immediately treated me like a guest at a dinner party.

"Mr. Martin?"

I nodded, as she pulled the rhinestone-rimmed glasses hanging from a pearl chain up into position.

"Good. Yes. I thought as much. It was nice of you to come."

She extended her right arm toward me almost as if she expected me to kiss her hand. I shook it, reaching up slightly to pull it down within normal range. Was she, as my grandmother used to say, putting on airs? Or had she taken to heart what she learned in a seminar on graciousness at a morticians' convention?

"Please come into the sitting room where we'll be more comfortable."

I followed her as she opened a heavy wooden door and led me into a huge room lined with bookshelves. All open spaces on the walls were filled with pictures of Spanish men in capes and women with mantillas; a few depicted children with bobbed hair wearing sashes, looking like miniature copies of the adults. I always appreciate rooms filled with books and feel a kinship with people who own and display them, so I took a detour in my walk to have a closer look. I was soon sorry that I did. The books were a combination of selections from the Reader's Digest Condensed Book Club and something called *The Annals of Undertaking*.

My hostess turned at that point, expecting me to be closer than I was. "Mr. Mar . . . Oh, there you are."

I rushed to her side. "I'm always interested in what people read. I'm a writer myself." This old ploy is usually good for a diversion from whatever I have done to offend someone or arouse their suspicions.

"A writer. How interesting."

Works every time.

"Let's sit here at my desk."

I leaped into a position where I could pull out her highbacked and uncomfortable-looking Spanish chair.

"Why, thank you, Mr. Martin."

I smiled and sat across the heavy-looking table with carvings of saints on the sides and legs. "I'm sorry. I told you my name, but didn't have the pleasure of getting yours." I was topping even myself in the niceness department. It all seemed hollow, but it was working wonderfully well.

"Oh, no. I beg your pardon. I'm Nadine Chapman. I own this mortuary in partnership with my husband, Lyle."

"Good to meet you," I said, half rising to my feet. She motioned for me to sit.

"Now, what can I do for you?"

"As I mentioned on the phone, my aunt has recently died and . . ."

"Please accept my utmost condolences."

"Thank you, I . . ."

"Were you close, I mean did she raise you from boyhood?"

Once in a while when I lie so outrageously, I get red in the face. I guess it's my conscience warning my mind to watch its step. I suddenly felt hot all over.

"Are you ill, Mr. Martin? You look as crimson as that candle."

"No, I guess it is warm in here—or maybe I'm coming down with something."

"Let me turn up the air conditioning."

She got up and walked a few feet to a thermostat and then resumed her seat across from me.

"Is that better? I hadn't realized how stuffy it was in here."

"Great. Feels much better. Thank you. Anyway, as I was saying, my aunt died and I was interested in finding out about your services for burial and cremation. I haven't decided which yet."

"And embalming. She must, by state law, be embalmed."

"Oh, of course. But that's already done. You see, she died in Portland, and a mortuary is handling that part up there."

"Oh, I see. Which one?"

"Offhand, I don't remember the name. I'll get back to you on that if we make an arrangement."

"I'm sure we will. We are the best on the central coast."

"I know you are."

We talked for a time about costs and types of funerals and plots and headstones.

"Could we take a tour? It's such an interesting-looking building. I'd like to see more."

"Of course."

She guided me beyond another heavy wooden door into a long, dimly lighted hall. Indistinct organ music drifted in and out, something between hymns and tunes played on a calliope.

"These are our slumber rooms," she said, gesturing right and left as we walked. We stepped through a door into a small patio—complete with another splashing fountain—surrounded by the building on all four sides. She motioned for me to follow her across to another massive door, flanked on both sides by stained-glass windows.

"Our chapel. Please come in."

As we stepped through the door, the organ music became louder. Wooden pews lined both sides of the main aisle, which extended to a large altar at the other end. More stained-glass windows filled one wall, and the tall ceiling had wooden beams stretching across it at various intervals. I could see an open coffin and banks of flowers placed in front of it.

"I won't go any farther. I don't want to disturb the dead."

"That's poor Mr. Jenkins, a retired fisherman. Services are tomorrow."

We stepped outside again. The sun reflected off the colorful windows and filled the patio with more light than you usually see on the Oregon coast.

"How many employees do you have?"

"Let's see, besides my husband and myself, there's Andrea, the night hostess, and three other morticians. Then two hearse drivers and Adam, a retarded man who keeps up the grounds and digs graves."

"What about security?"

"Well, we lock the gates at night and this building, of course. I'm sure your aunt will be quite safe with us. Then, too, Adam has a small cottage next to the mausoleum at the far end of the grounds. He's instructed to call 911 if he hears anything. That is, if he would know enough to do that." She looked around. "He's not very bright. He's only working here because my husband did a favor for a friend. But you're not interested in all my gossip, I'm sure."

Don't bet on it, I thought to myself. "So he stays there all night?"

"Yes, sir, except when he's off, and then I guess he visits his mother up in Depoe Bay."

I had everything I had come for and more. It was time to put an end to my little charade.

"You've been more than kind to give me so much of your time." I extended my hand.

"My pleasure, Mr. Martin. Oh, there's my husband." She was looking behind me toward the main part of the building. "I know he'll want to meet you. Lyle . . ."

A tall, thin man came toward us across the patio. With his pale skin and black suit, he looked, I hate to say it, like a cadaver.

"Mr. Martin's a new client. His aunt has died, and he's looking us over as a potential final resting place for his loved one. I told him . . ."

Chapman put up his hand to stop his wife's endless chattering. He'd probably been listening to much of the same for many years.

" . . . more than he wanted to know," he said, smiling at me and acting as if she weren't there. "I'm sure, Mr. Martin, is it?" he turned to me.

I nodded.

" . . . Mr. Martin needs to make up his mind in peace. We won't keep you."

"Lyle, that's rude."

"Shut up, Nadine. I'm handling this."

Never one to ignore a personal slight or perceived insult, I answered in kind. "I wasn't aware that I needed handling."

He disregarded what I said and began moving me toward the main building.

"I can make it on my own," I said, raising an arm to ward off his hold on me. Nadine just stood there, a perplexed look on her face.

"Lyle . . . Lyle! Why are you doing this?"

He ignored her and kept nudging me along. I was surprised by his treatment. I was an imposter, of course, but there was no way he could know that. I hadn't told anyone I was coming here or what I was looking for. Hell, I wasn't sure what I was looking for, so how could this gruesome man know? I wanted to ask him if he'd been at the lighthouse, but hesitated.

"Look, Mr. Chapman. I'll be happy to take my business elsewhere."

"I doubt there is any business to take," he answered.

How could he see into my mind? I didn't reply, but turned abruptly and retraced my steps across the grand salon, the foyer, and out the front door. I got into my car and drove away quickly, the formaldehyde/pine scent still in my nostrils.

I waited until dark to return. It was the cemetery I was interested in, not the mortuary; I had seen enough of that depressing and pretentious building to last a lifetime. I wanted to have a look at the cottage where Adam Edwards lived. I didn't expect him to be there, but I thought I might see something that would help me find him. The police had probably already searched the place. But, you never know.

At just after ten, I parked my car in a small wayside off Highway 101. It wouldn't take me long to walk the quarter mile to the cemetery, and it was a warm night with only a slight breeze blowing up from the ocean.

On my first visit, I had noticed a grove of shore pines adjoining the cemetery property to the south. As I walked around a metal barrier to enter, I noticed—on the "No Trespassing" sign posted nearby—that it was owned by a timber company. I felt perfectly safe using the forest to make my entrance and exit to the cemetery.

When I reached the boundary, I stopped to get a feel for the place. Straight ahead lay rows and rows of grave stones glistening in the moonlight. Adam was doing a good job of keeping the cemetery well maintained; the grass was cut and even trimmed around the stones. I could see the hacienda at the far end of the property. A single light was on in a lower window, probably so Chapman could see to get into his Dracula costume. "How-do-you-do, my dear," I said aloud in my best Bela Lugosi imitation.

To my right on a slight incline sat two buildings, one which I was sure was where Adam Edwards stayed when he was not being sought by the police for murder.

"Poor guy," I muttered under my breath. Did he even know they were looking for him? And what would happen when they found him?

I walked up the hill and reached the buildings in a few seconds. The first was a metal shed, probably to house lawn mowers and leaf blowers and other equipment. A padlock held the only door firmly in place.

The other building was identical to the first except for the conventional door and window that replaced the larger overhead door on the storage shed. Adam's cottage looked more like a garage. I tried the door, but it wouldn't budge. The window was locked, too. I walked around to the back wall where I found another window. Luckily, it was up about an inch from the bottom. I reached up and opened it as wide as possible.

From the ground, it looked small. I wanted to think that my long, lanky frame could get through the opening, but I wasn't so sure. There was also the distance from the ground to the window—it was too great to climb without a ladder or something.

I switched on my flashlight and scanned the area. At first, nothing looked promising, but then I spotted what looked like unused grave markers strewn around farther up the hill. Apparently Chapman's operation wasn't so tidy behind the scenes.

The stones were easy to move to the side of the building. When I stacked ten of them, one on top of the other, I had my ladder. I climbed onto the makeshift platform and was able to get the leverage I needed to maneuver my body headfirst through the window.

I emerged half in and half out over a bathtub and hung there for a moment like I was flying, then grabbed a sturdy towel rack and pulled myself in. My feet dropped with a thud into the tub, and I got out gingerly. The bathroom smelled as if it hadn't been cleaned in a long time, but I didn't turn on the light to see for certain. Instead, I moved into the only other room in the building, and risked turning on my flashlight to scan the place.

An unmade bed was to my right with a small metal wardrobe standing next to it. A bookcase full of seashells, rocks, glass fishing floats, and other beachcombing souvenirs dotted its shelves, but no books were in sight. A sagging armchair with torn upholstery sat next to it. In the center of the room was a table with two chairs, one on each side. It was covered with papers and plastic models of all kinds: boats, airplanes, old cars, logging trucks. Several containers of glue sat nearby. Adam apparently spent his idle hours making models. I was glad he had found something he enjoyed doing, but felt sad if this was all he had to look forward to in life.

I sat at the table to look through the pile of papers. Most were directions for making this model or that. When he had finished one, he hadn't bothered to clear away the debris before starting another.

In the middle of the pile, I found a heartbreaking note: a list of "Things to Do Each Day," which had apparently been given to Adam by his mother:

- *Get up*
- *Go to toilet*
- *Take a shower*
- *Brush teeth*

- *Comb hair*
- *Put on clothes, underwear first*
- *Put on socks*
- *Put on shoes (boots if a rainy day)*
- *Eat something (don't try to cook—buy something)*
- *Go to work*

At night:
- *Eat something (don't try to cook—buy something)*
- *Brush teeth*
- *Go to toilet*
- *Get undressed and ready for bed*
- *Go to bed*

Note: You don't have to take a shower at night or comb your hair

Next to the list was a wide space and a grid pattern to allow Adam to place a check mark next to each activity after he had completed it. For the first few days, he had checked off everything. Then, perhaps growing tired of this tedious process, he had skipped things here and there: no bath one day, no teeth brushing or hair combing the next. He had probably gotten the idea of what to do from this list, but just not recorded it.

The list made me admire Rose Edwards. It said a lot about how caring she was and the stress Adam's situation must have caused her for years. I doubted that very many people could cope with all she had encountered in her life.

I put the list back on the table, then opened a small drawer. It held items you might find in a young boy's pocket: string, a top, a toy soldier, an Indian arrowhead, some sea shells, and a smooth stone—his good luck piece. On a hunch, I took the drawer out and lifted it up to see if anything was taped to the underside. A key had been clumsily affixed to the wood with a Band-Aid. I pealed it loose and examined it more closely. It looked like it would fit a padlock. On it, someone had scratched the letters RQ.

"Rock quarry at Yaquina Head," I muttered to myself. Adam Edwards's hideout. I slipped the key into my pocket and put the drawer back in place.

Just then I heard voices outside. I closed the drawer slowly, then stepped back into the only possible hiding place in this tiny house—the bathroom. As I hid behind the half-open door, the glint of two flashlights reflected on the glass. Soon, I heard the sound of a key turning in the lock. I quickly and quietly closed the bathroom door.

"God damn imbecile. I don't think he's here." Lyle Chapman, the creepy mortician. "Come on in. I'll turn on the light."

The room was suddenly flooded with the harsh glow of fluorescent tubes sputtering above.

"God, what a mess."

I couldn't see the other person with Chapman from my hiding place and didn't feel I had better try.

"Are you sure the kid overheard you?" The other man. The voice sounded vaguely familiar, but I couldn't place it.

"Yeah, no question. I found him crouched down in the patio outside my office a couple days ago. It was when you called me about that French lady's house."

Simone. What possible interest could Chapman have in her?

"But he wouldn't be able to tell anything by just hearing one side of a conversation."

"You're right, but I was stupid enough to have the speakerphone on. What you said echoed all over the room."

"You mean about my getting her to sell the house to me so you could turn it into a mortuary?"

"That's exactly what I mean. That's why I'm worried about Adam. If he tells his mother . . ."

"He can't tell her anything if he's dead, by golly." Verne Andrews, Simone's attorney. That was why he seemed to be pressuring her to sell the house when I overheard them at the brunch.

In spite of my current predicament, I smiled to myself as I pictured the two of them standing together: Buffalo Bill meets Count Dracula.

"You're as slow as he is, Verne, if you think I'm going to kill him over a single real estate transaction. If you had done what you bragged about doing, we wouldn't be in this mess right now."

"Sure, blame me, Lyle. I wasn't the one who botched things up when we . . ."

My foot shifted just enough for the floor to creak.

"Hear that?" Chapman interrupted. "Maybe that little jerk's been hiding in the bathroom all along."

He stepped toward the door and rattled the knob.

"Adam. It's Mr. Lyle. Come on out and see me. I won't hurt you. I just want to tell you a story."

As quietly as I could, I reached down and snapped the lock into place. It wouldn't hold the flimsy door closed for very long, but it might give me a few seconds to get out of there.

Both men were throwing their weight against the bathroom door, but the lock held. I looked frantically for some place to hide.

I hadn't noticed a large built-in cupboard behind me. I opened the door and found that its shelves had been removed to make it into a closet. I got down on my hands and knees to pry open a screen that covered the bottom. This must have once been a cooler used to store food or other perishable supplies, with the screen allowing air from underneath the building to circulate into the cupboard. The old wooden frame gave way easily. I dropped feet first through the opening, pulling the screen back into place once I had gained my footing.

All the while, Chapman was yelling, "Adam, I know you're in there. Open the door."

I moved away from the opening and crawled toward what I thought was the way out. Once there, I could see the outside world through the wooden lattice skirt that covered the bottom of the building. I kicked a hole in the lattice at about the same time I heard the men break through the bathroom door.

I scrambled out and headed toward the woods. I didn't stop running until I reached my car, then I drove south in search of a place to have some coffee and collect my thoughts.

Nothing was open until I got to Waldport, a logging and fishing town about fifteen miles south of Newport. I stopped at a café there to decide what to do next.

"Menu?"

The waitress was middle-aged and motherly looking in her yellow uniform and starched cap. A large lacy handkerchief cascaded from her pocket. Her name tag read La Donna.

"Yes. Thanks."

I realized I hadn't eaten since lunch and was feeling light-headed.

"Coffee in the meantime?"

"Please. I know what I want," I said, closing the menu and handing it back to her. She stood with her pen poised. "A short stack with bacon."

"Maple or marionberry syrup?"

"Maple, please."

She wrote down my order, then walked behind the counter to shout it to the invisible cook in the kitchen. The café was empty, although I could see an unfinished meal complete with a half-filled and still steaming coffee cup on a nearby table. Someone had interrupted a meal to go to the rest room. I gazed out the window at the highway where traffic was practically nonexistent at this hour. A minute later, I could feel someone standing next to my table before I fixed on his reflection in the window.

"Well, well, well. Fancy meeting you here."

My heart sank. Sheriff Kutler in civilian clothes.

"Hello, sheriff. I didn't think you ever took off your badge of office."

"Once in a while, professor."

I smiled benignly, deciding that it would be better not to bait him. I gritted my teeth and tried to act pleasant.

"Just a minute, I'll join you."

Before I could object, he picked up his plate, cup, and eating utensils and sat down, resuming his meal—an omelet and fried potatoes.

"La Donna," he signaled to the waitress. "More coffee."

He turned to me and smiled, pieces of egg in his teeth. I drank some coffee, wishing for food of my own to occupy me so I wouldn't betray my nervousness. Fortunately, La Donna brought my meal when she came to refill the cups with coffee. After slathering the pancakes with butter, I picked up the pitcher and poured some syrup. Kutler watched me intently, as if trying to catch me in a mistake.

"Marionberry's better."

"What?"

"Marionberry syrup. It goes better with hot cakes."

I poured more maple syrup on the pancakes in a gesture of defiance.

"What brings you so far south?"

"I was driving back from a poetry reading in Yachats."

Yachats was a town ten miles farther south that was rapidly becoming artsy and bookish because of events held all summer. I had guessed about the public reading and hoped Kutler wouldn't check.

"That's how your shirt got so dirty? Poetry come with a little mud wrestlin'?" He laughed at his own joke, then looked under the table. "And your pants?"

"I have to confess I couldn't resist stopping along the way to walk along the beach. I just don't do that nearly enough."

Kutler looked skeptical, but didn't say any more about it. That was nothing new. Kutler always looked skeptical. I cleaned my plate before speaking again.

"I have to ask, sheriff—have you found out who killed my friend Simone Godard?"

"That's for me to know and you to find out."

Kutler had been congenial until this point, but this remark made me realize what a jerk he really was. I dropped the subject because I knew further questions would only result in more smart-ass answers. For his part, however, Kutler wanted to tell me what he had found out. He just wanted me to pry it out of him. He finished eating and pushed his plate away, signaling the waitress.

"Hey, sweet thing. Bring me a piece of that bananer cream pie."

She bustled around the counter, taking a clean plate from a shelf and opening the glass case to remove a large pie pan. She cut him a generous piece and hurried over with it.

"Here you are, hon. More coffee?"

Kutler nodded and stroked her arm as he smiled up at her.

I put my hand over my cup to ward off another refill. At this point my kidneys were already floating. I started making moves in preparation for leaving—gathering my glasses, getting out my wallet, looking at the bill.

"Are you leaving me, old buddy?" Kutler said, his mouth full of pie.

"If you were really my buddy, sheriff, you'd tell me about your investigation."

"Okay. Okay. Hold your horses while I finish eating." That he did in two large mouthfuls. "Great stuff, but a little hard on the waistline," he said, pointing to a large roll of fat protruding more than a little bit over his belt.

"Oh, you'll soon work that off chasing bad guys," I replied cheerfully.

"We still think Adam Edwards killed your friend."

Now it was my turn to be skeptical. "I don't know him at all—never met him—but it doesn't seem likely to me that a mentally retarded man could form that kind of rage—I mean enough to kill someone who had a history of helping him and who was his mother's boss."

Kutler didn't like being contradicted. His mood changed abruptly into the nasty man I had grown to dislike ten years ago.

"So, now you're a detective. You smart guys slay me, Martindale. You think just because you got a few academic degrees in back of your name you know it all." Kutler's voice was rising. Even La Donna—busy washing glasses behind the counter—looked up.

"Look, sheriff. I'm sorry you aren't highly educated. I'm sorry you resent people like me who have college degrees. But the failures of your past aren't my fault."

At the word failure, Kutler looked as if I had slugged him. I didn't wait for a reply, but got up and walked to the register. La Donna hurried up to collect my money.

"That'll be $5.40," she said loudly, then dropped her voice to a whisper. "I don't know what's goin' on between you and Art, but I'd be careful about makin' him mad. Art's not a good enemy to have."

"Here's ten dollars," I said loudly, but adding in a whisper, "Thanks for the warning."

I raised my voice for the grand exit. "Keep the change." I turned to Kutler, who was red in the face. "Watch your blood pressure and your cholesterol, sheriff. That stuff will kill you." Saying that, I walked out the door and shut it so hard I could hear the little bell attached to it still ringing even after I was in my car.

I made good time from Waldport to Newport because traffic at this late hour was light. I spent the time trying to decide whether to go back to Yaquina Head and look for Adam Edwards's shack. I was certain he was hiding there. I was also fairly certain Kutler knew nothing about that. Otherwise, he wouldn't have been calmly eating pie in Waldport.

All the way up the highway I kept looking in my rearview mirror, half expecting Kutler to follow me—for harassment reasons if nothing else. But the view behind me was dark. Nevertheless, I still watched my speedometer to make sure I stayed within the speed limit.

In my concentration on the plight of Adam Edwards, however, I neglected to think about police radios—or to realize that the sheriff wouldn't need to pull me over himself. Just after I got over the Yaquina Bay Bridge, flashing lights loomed behind me. I pulled over to the side and got my license and registration ready.

I didn't see that the man had his gun drawn until he pointed it in my face.

Keep your hands in plain sight and get out of the vehicle," he ordered. It was another sheriff's deputy.

"I don't get it, officer. What did I do to . . ."

"Get out, get out, get out. Now." He was getting agitated, a younger version of Art Kutler. What had the sheriff told him about me?

I slowly eased out, hands in the air, one still holding the license and registration, both seeming superfluous now.

"I don't get . . ."

"Shut up and assume the position."

"What position?"

He turned me around and slammed my hands against the car with such force that my documents fluttered to the ground. Then, in the time-honored fashion I had seen so many times in movies and television shows, he patted me down in a search for weapons. Finding nothing, he turned me around, eyes flashing.

"May I pick up my stuff?" I asked, motioning to the documents now lying close to the opening of a storm drain.

He nodded and I bent down. When I retrieved the two pieces of paper, I started to stand up, but suddenly felt a blow to my neck. I'd never studied karate, but the swiftness of the hit showed me how lethal it can be. I fell forward on all fours, wondering what would happen next. La Donna the waitress had been right: it wasn't a good idea to make Sheriff Kutler angry.

As I braced for another blow—a kick this time, perhaps—I spotted the flashing lights of another vehicle and heard the short burst of a siren as it pulled to a stop. I stayed where I was, wondering in my dizzy state whether Kutler had arrived to finish the job his deputy had started.

"What's going on here, deputy? Is this World War III or what?"

It wasn't Kutler's semi-literate voice, but the unmistakable cadences of Brooklyn, New York—World War III had sounded like *World Wah Tree*.

The deputy started to sputter a reply. "I pulled him over for speeding, and he started giving me trouble so I . . ."

"Gave him a lesson in who's the boss?" said the new voice.

By this time I was lying flat on the ground with my head turned to the left. Soon, a pair of polished boots stopped just beyond my nose. I turned my head and followed the legs up to a belt, a holster, a gun and a kind face peering anxiously down at me. His name tag said Golden, a name that didn't register in my, by then, addled brain.

"Are you okay, sir? Let me help you up."

He tugged on my left arm, and I got to my feet. The deputy had walked back to the patrol car, lights still flashing. I faced my rescuer, my relief surely showing on my face. He was a sergeant in the Oregon State Police. He took my license and examined it longer than necessary.

"Thomas Martindale. Are you heading home?" He was talking

loudly for the benefit of the now sulking deputy. Golden moved closer to me as he handed me the license. "I'm a friend of Angela Pride. Be cool, and I'll get you out of this," he whispered.

"Please get back in your vehicle, sir."

I did as I was told, feeling a combination of relief that he had saved me and anger that I had gotten into this predicament in the first place. Golden walked back to the deputy, and they talked for a few minutes. At first the sheriff's man gestured wildly and kept shaking his head. Golden seemed just as firm in his responses, looking down at the shorter man and punctuating his words with a pointed finger now and again.

Finally, the deputy threw up his hands and stomped to his car. He got in, slammed the door loudly, and sped off, glancing at me in contempt as he roared by. I watched in the side mirror as Golden walked up.

"Can I buy you some coffee back at headquarters? It'll be a better place to talk," he said.

"Sure. I'll follow you anywhere you want—the moon, Canada, you name it. You saved my bacon."

"Not to mention your ass," he laughed.

He walked to his car and pulled out onto Highway 101. I followed him as closely as I could without our bumpers touching. I felt a lot of comfort in the knowledge that someone was helping me.

The Newport district office of the Oregon State Police was housed in a new building several miles north of the city limits. I had gotten familiar with the inside of the old facility ten years ago when Angela had helped me clear an old girlfriend of murder. On the drive north, I remembered that Nate Golden was the officer she said I could call on for help.

We turned onto a side road and then drove into the fenced enclosure in front of the OSP building. I locked my car and followed Golden inside. No one was at the reception desk as we passed into a long hall. The sergeant motioned me into a dark office on the left, while reaching in to turn on the harsh overhead light.

"I'll get the coffee. Is black all right with you? I'm sure we're out of milk at this hour."

"Sure. Not coffee regular."

He stopped and looked at me, a smile on his face.

"You've lived in New York?"

"For two years about twenty years ago."

In that arrogance that only New Yorkers possess, coffee regular means coffee with milk, something every vendor and waitress will give you without fail unless you specify coffee black. He soon returned with two cups.

"I don't meet very many people here who've ever lived there. I'm kind of an oddity."

"How'd you wind up here?"

"I was an exchange student at Portland State, and I like living in Oregon." He pronounced it *Ory-gone*, a common mistake that makes most Oregonians angry.

"I'm surprised they let you stay if you say the name of their state that way," I laughed, half-serious. Oregonians can be flinty at times about little things.

"Yeah, I know what you mean."

"How'd you meet Angela Pride?"

"In Salem when I was training. She gave several lectures there, and then we've met a lot since I took over the job here. Before she became head of security at the university, she worked out of this office, but I guess you know that."

"Oh, yeah. Angela and I go a long way back, and our friendship began right here in this room." I sipped some coffee. "What did she tell you about me?"

"She said you were a friend and to help you if I could." He paused.

"And? Go ahead, Sergeant Golden . . ."

"Please call me Nate."

"Okay, Nate. Tell me what else she said. You won't offend me."

"She said you sometimes got carried away while trying to help people and that you also think of yourself as some kind of private eye because you used to be an investigative reporter for a magazine before you started teaching." He seemed uneasy to be ratting on his superior and stopped talking to watch my reaction and take a sip of coffee.

"Angela's got me all figured out," I laughed. "I'm sure I've been a real pain in the ass to her at times, but she always comes through for me."

My relaxed response seemed to put Golden at ease, and he got more expansive.

"She also said she sometimes had to save you from yourself."

"Now, that I'm not sure I agree with," I responded.

He seemed chagrined at having spoken so frankly. I couldn't believe how nice a guy he was.

We both took sips of coffee and didn't speak for a few moments.

"At any rate," I broke the silence, "I'm grateful for her help and for your being there tonight. I'd rather not think about what else that deputy had in mind for me. How'd you happen to come along?"

"I don't usually get night duty, but one of my troopers called in sick so I decided to fill in for him at the last minute. I was just driving down 101 when I saw the deputy pull you over. We've gotten a few complaints lately about that. So I decided to have a look. When I heard your name over the radio, I thought I'd better step in."

"It was my lucky night."

"So, why do you think Sheriff Kutler has it in for you?"

"About ten years ago—the same time I met Angela—I was trying to help an old girlfriend clear her name. She was accused of murdering one of the scientists at the Marine Center."

"Was that the case involving whales?"

I nodded.

"I won't bore you with the details now, but Kutler thought Susan—my friend—was guilty and really resented it when I eventually cleared her. I also turned him in for blowing up a whale and, because of all the publicity, he was ousted in the next election. He ran again later and won. I guess people forgive and forget."

"Oh, is that all?" he laughed. "I thought it was something serious."

I filled him in on Kutler and the dead whale, and he sat there smiling. "That was in the past. Why's he on your case so much now?"

I recounted most of what had happened: Simone's death, Adam as a suspect, and my run-ins with Kutler at both my house and the café in Waldport. I left out the parts about my so-called undercover work.

"There are no other suspects in her death, I mean besides this Edwards guy?"

"That's just the problem. Like before, Kutler has fixated on one person to the exclusion of everyone else."

"Well, who are the other possibilities? I'll take a look at them."

"I don't have a list. I don't want to accuse anyone unjustly. I just don't want Adam to get hurt. He's, well, slow and I'm not sure what he'd do if the police rushed in."

"They'll have to find him to rush in on him, Tom. I gather he's missing?"

I nodded.

"So, where's he live?"

"A little house at the cemetery where he works. I guess he hangs out where his mother works, too. She is—was—the housekeeper for my friend who was killed."

"Right, the French lady. He's got no other place to go?"

I wasn't about to tell Golden about the shack at the rock quarry. I liked him and was grateful to him, but not enough to trust him completely. He was, after all, a policeman before everything else. "Not that I know of, no."

"If you hear anything about him, let me know, okay?"

"Sure. You bet."

I stifled a yawn with my hand.

"I'm fading fast. Not used to these late hours, I guess." I stood up and extended my hand. We shook heartily. "Nate. Thank you very much for coming to my aid. I really appreciate your help. I hope I won't have to call on you again, but it eases my mind to know that I can if I need to."

"Absolutely, Tom. Anytime. Here's my cell phone number. Call anytime."

I turned toward the door. "Thanks. I can find my way out."

"Tom?"

I stopped, putting his card in my pocket.

"Keep out of Sheriff Kutler's way. Don't give him any excuse to hassle you again. Promise?"

"You bet, Nate. I wouldn't think of it."

Wednesday

I slept late the next morning, exhausted from the events of the night before. After showering and breakfast, I called Rose Edwards.

"Good morning, Rose. Tom Martindale calling."

"Oh, Mr. Martindale. Have you found my Adam?"

I had decided not to say anything to her yet about finding the key to the shack.

"I'm afraid not. Has he called you?"

"No, but at least he's not a suspect anymore."

"Why do you say that?"

"A story in our local paper."

"What do you mean?'

"*The Depoe Bay Whaler.* It's kind of a joke around here. Mostly ads. But it prints a few news stories. Wait, let me get it."

I could hear her footsteps, then a rustling of paper as she returned and picked up to receiver.

"Here it is. There's a story about Madame Godard's death, and it doesn't say anything about Adam."

"Go on. Read it to me. What does it say?"

"I didn't read it all."

"Would you mind reading it to me?" I was trying to keep the edge out of my voice, but was beginning to get impatient as she started to read, clearing her throat as if she was making a radio broadcast.

"Prominent professor found dead in cove. That's the headline. The body of a retired professor of French at the university washed ashore in Whale Cove Tuesday. Simone Godard, who lived in retirement on Point Avenue in Depoe Bay, disappeared early Monday, according to a spokesman for County Sheriff Art Kutler. The investigation is continuing, but there were no new leads at press time. Police have questioned several possible suspects, including Thomas Martindale, a journalism professor who was a friend of Godard. Martindale has a home in Newport."

"Who wrote this piece of garbage?"

"Let's see. . . ." The paper rustled again. "Someone named Charles Gates."

Why didn't it surprise me that my old nemesis from the University of Oregon and the Fred Meyer wine department was behind this—with assistance from my pal Sheriff Kutler, of course.

"So, you think Adam's in the clear just because he wasn't mentioned?"

"Well, yes. I guess I do. Don't you agree?"

"I wish things in life were that simple, Rose. I know this writer. He's trying to embarrass me. That's what this story is about, nothing more."

"What are you going to do, Mr. Martindale?"

"Try to scare the owner of this paper into printing a retraction, first of all."

"I wondered if you'd help me, too?"

"What'd you have in mind?"

"Fred Bader. I think you met him at the brunch."

"Yes. Simone's German colleague. What's he up to?"

"He called last night, and I'm afraid I said too much about what happened."

"What do you mean?"

"I'm afraid I told him about the study—about the vandalism and the swastika."

"Oh, that's too bad. I wanted to get the state police on that."

"When I told Mr. Bader what happened, he said he'd come over and help me clean it up. He's got that relative visiting from Germany, and he's coming over to the coast today to rent a house and said he'd stop up."

"That wouldn't be a good idea. When's he supposed to be there?"

"About noon."

"Look, Rose, I'll be there before then. Don't let him into the study. I'll get a friend with the state police to have a look at it."

"Thank you, Mr. Martindale. I'll even fix you some lunch."

I hung up and called Nate Golden on his cell phone, getting him out of the shower. I explained what had happened, and he agreed to meet me at the Godard house at noon. Before I got there, however, I had a stop to make in Depoe Bay at the offices of a certain newspaper.

In my cursory glances at it, *The Depoe Bay Whaler* looked like a typical weekly newspaper: long on ads and local gossip, short on anything that resembled real journalism. Its offices were housed in a small building on U.S. 101, which was the town's main drag as well as being an often crowded Federal highway.

As I got out of my car and headed toward the newspaper office, I was almost knocked down by two men coming out of the building next door.

"Watch where you're going, pal," said the portlier of the two.

"I could say the same for . . ." I started to say, when I realized it was Simone's attorney, Verne Andrews, and Lyle Chapman, the mortician. I glanced at the sign on the wall: Andrews and Associates, Attorneys at Law. Office Upstairs. "Mr. Andrews. Tom Martindale. We met at Simone Godard's brunch last week."

The big man's hostility quickly turned to sorrow, as if on cue from an invisible director. "Poor See-moan," he dragged out her name as before. "Her death's a big loss for us all."

Chapman had been studying me as his friend talked. As before, he was wearing black. "Haven't we met?" he said finally.

"I don't think so," I lied, surprised that he hadn't remembered. "What brings the two of you together? Working out the details to turn Simone's house into a mortuary?" I had decided to say something daring to get their attention. My technique worked, perhaps too well. They both looked startled, especially Andrews.

"How did you . . ."

"We're late for lunch, Verne," interrupted Chapman, who had kept his cool. He pulled Andrews away.

"Did you bury your poor aunt, Mr. Martindale?" he said over his shoulder, as they hurried down the sidewalk. He had remembered me.

I then stepped into the newspaper office, entering a room that was small and unremarkable except for the piles of past issues strewn around on folding chairs, the floor, and a long counter running the length of the back wall. The air was heavy with the scent of newsprint and ink that many people in journalism claim entices them into the business. Not me. I prefer the clean air of a magazine office where the printing press is not in the back room. Ink-stained—or ink-smelling—wretches are as out-dated in journalism as green eyeshades and spittoons.

I walked to the end of the counter, away from two waiting customers. As angry as I was about the story, I was willing to wait my turn. I picked up a copy of the latest edition of the paper and read the story. As I stood contemplating what I would say to the owner of this rag, I glanced at the two people. An older woman was talking earnestly to a younger man who was wearing a soft-drink company uniform. He looked embarrassed about whatever she was saying. She was gazing into his eyes and laughing. When she suddenly turned to stare at me, he seemed relieved and hurried out the door.

"Tom. Tom Martindale," she shouted, jarring both me and the harried-looking clerk on duty.

I focused on a middle-aged woman wearing a purple leotard and a yellow sequin-covered smock. Understated attire was not in her fashion manual. As our eyes met, she looked vaguely familiar, but only that.

"You bad boy," she said, walking over to me so fast her orange platform shoes made clopping sounds on the worn linoleum. She grabbed me and hugged me tightly. I didn't pull away, but I didn't embrace her in return, wishing I was someplace else.

"Don't you remember me?" she asked, looking crestfallen.

"Of course, I do," I lied. "It is good to see you again." I was using the politician's obfuscation to buy a few minutes to think. The cogs and wheels in my brain were desperately turning, trying to connect to the proper name in whatever niche it was momentarily hiding.

"I'm so glad. I'd have been crushed to think you'd forgotten me so soon."

The woman behind the counter looked from one of us to the other, and back again, probably imagining all kinds of licentious encounters involving chains and leather and orange platform shoes.

I didn't say a word, but that didn't matter, because my new-found friend was moving things along just fine.

"Oh, poor Simone," she said, holding one hand over her heart and fanning herself with the other one.

My mind settled on the quarry: friend of Simone, I'd met her at the house. At that point her name rolled into place.

"Yes, Connie. It's terrible."

This was Connie Wright, who had been next to me at the brunch. She had been introduced as someone who served on the symphony board. Hearing me say her name, Connie dabbed at her eyes and actually put her head on my shoulder. The woman behind the counter raised an eyebrow. I chanced the placement of one hand on her shoulder, both to give a comforting pat and to push her gently away. The counter woman looked away and busied herself with some papers.

"I intended to call you," Connie said. "I've got some things Simone gave me for safekeeping. You see, I've got a safe in my house for jewelry and papers. She gave me something several weeks ago—papers, I guess. Whatever it is, the envelope has your name on it. She wanted you to have it if anything happened to her."

"She said that?"

"She did. I thought she was just being melodramatic. Of course, I hadn't had the pleasure of meeting you then."

The woman behind the counter looked at me and winked. I quickly turned away and tried to camouflage the shudder that ran through my body.

"Well, where is the envelope now?"

"In my safe, ready for you to pick up. Why don't you come by for drinks tonight." The look in her eyes reflected sheer determination. I could tell I was not going to get Simone's envelope easily.

"Sure. I'd be happy to come over."

"How thrilling. I enjoy you."

Her use of the word "enjoy" brought both eyebrows up on the face of the woman behind the counter. For an instant, I saw myself bound and gagged, Connie Wright looming over me with knife and fork.

" . . . I mean your company," she added, glancing nervously for the first time at the now smirking counter woman. Connie then raised an arm heavily laden with jingling bracelets and looked at her watch. "I've got to be going. I've got a lot of do to get ready for tonight."

"Ma'am," the woman behind the counter spoke for the first time. "Your ad?"

Connie looked puzzled. "Oh, yes. I forgot—in all the excitement." She turned to me. "I was placing an ad to announce the fall season for our little local symphony here. You'll want to come as my guest." Connie Wright was already planning our second date.

She pulled a wallet out of her handbag. "How much, Wanda?"

"Forty-three dollars and eighty cents for two issues."

"Here you are. I'll need a receipt." She started tapping her foot, suddenly impatient even though she had wasted fifteen minutes with her prattle. It was going to be a long evening.

"Where do you live, Connie?"

"Oh, of course." She pulled a card out of her purse. "It's in Miroco, a small community just north of the top of Cape Foulweather."

"I know where that is. What time?"

"Seven o'clock. I'll have a little something for us to eat."

I nodded, as she took her change and turned toward the door.

"See you then, dear," she said cheerfully, raising her arm to wave, infernal bracelets jingling. She whisked out and got into a brown Jaguar parked at the curb. I turned to the woman behind the counter.

"Ms. Wright's a good cook," she said.

"That'll be something to look forward to," I answered grimly.

"You wanted to place an ad?"

"I wanted to see the owner. Tom Martindale is my name."

"That would be Mr. Gates. Mr. Merle Gates."

Chuck Gates's uncle, who had given his ne'er-do-well nephew a job and was about to be sued for libel.

"And you are . . . Mr. Martingale?"

"Dale. Martin-dale."

"Can I tell him what this is in regards to?"

"A complaint."

She walked back through a swinging door, and I got a glimpse of Chuck Gates standing there looking out at me, a goofy grin on his face. He had probably heard everything, but I decided to save my wrath for his uncle.

Wanda reappeared in the doorway and motioned for me to follow. "Mr. Gates will see you now."

I found myself in a long room filled with everything a weekly newspaper needed: a few people working at computers and talking on the telephone, other people standing in front of lighted layout tables pasting up pages for the next issue. I could hear the sounds of a printing press in another room at the rear. Chuck Gates had disappeared.

Wanda took me to what seemed to be the only private office in the building, just next to a door marked "Press Room." As I reached the doorway, a small wiry man without a hair on his head was rising from his chair and walking around a table that served as his desk, his right hand extended.

"Mr. Merle Gates. This is Thomas Martingale."

"Martin-dale," I mumbled the correction.

Wanda moved aside to let me in.

Gates gripped my hand firmly. He looked to be in his seventies.

"As in Nightingale? Unusual name. I only recall hearing one other person named that. The nurse . . ." he paused and rubbed his chin.

"Florence."

"Oh, ha, my boy. That's it. Did you know her?"

Good grief. No wonder Gates had been able to run the story about me. His uncle was losing—or had already lost—it.

"No. I'm not as old as I look," I replied, not wanting to embarrass this seemingly innocent old man. "Actually, sir, my name is Martin-dale. D-A-L-E. Why don't you call me Tom?"

"Very well, Tom. I've never been very good with names. Sit down, sit down."

He motioned toward a wonderful oak chair that was probably only slightly older than he was. We faced each other across the battered old table. Behind him was a rolltop desk, its many cubbyholes stuffed with slips of paper.

"Now, what can I do for you?"

"I came in to complain about an error in a story in this week's issue." As I started to explain, I unrolled the paper I had tucked under my arm and folded it so he could see the offending story more easily. "It's right here: Prominent professor found dead in cove . . ."

"Not the best headline I've ever read," he said, "but better than those heads that begin with a verb like "Throw girl in river" or "Kill man in car wreck." That's tabloid writing, and I won't have it in my paper. But I'm boring you. You probably don't know anything about how headlines are written."

"Actually, I do, Mr. Gates. I teach journalism at Oregon University."

"The U of O? Well, why didn't you say so? I'm in the presence of a real expert. You could probably teach me and my people a great deal about headlines and writing."

"No, I teach at the other university."

"The hell, you say. That's the cow college. There's no journalism taught there. Just things about breeding chickens and cows and raising wheat. Did you know the flea collar was invented by a professor from there?"

"Yes, I did, and the maraschino cherry."

"Do tell. I didn't know that."

I could feel a major headache forming in the area behind my eyes. "The story, Mr. Gates."

"Very well, my boy. Go on."

"In the copy, it mentions me in passing as a suspect in a possible murder. I am the only person mentioned. I'm not sure how much you know about libel law, but in only a cursory reading of this, I think I have a very good case to sue you, the paper, and the reporter for libel."

The old man blinked repeatedly and got very pale. I kept my voice steady and my manner unthreatening. I didn't want him to have a heart attack.

"The byline says Charles Gates."

"Yes. He's my nephew, the son of my oldest sister, Bernice. He's had some bad luck lately. I gave him a job selling ads on commission, against my better judgment. I mean, he usually looks terrible—all that scraggly hair and wild beard. We had a long talk about that. He promised to shave and get a haircut, but then he didn't. Then he asked me if he could start doing some writing, and I let him. He's written before—some kind of PR job at the U of O in Eugene. I agreed because I thought he'd stand out less as a reporter than an ad salesman." He paused and stared into space. I kept quiet, hoping to hear something I didn't already know.

"He left there. Never told me why. But I wanted to help him out all I could—because of Bernice, you see. Chuck . . . come in here," he shouted. He was looking more miserable by the minute. Perhaps it was dawning on him that I could bring real trouble to his little paper.

"Didn't you read his copy?" I asked.

"At first I did, yes. But then I turned him out on his own. He did a few feature stories on that damned whale before it left."

"Keiko?"

"Yes. He got to know his way around the aquarium in Newport quite well. Did you ever hear of anything so ridiculous as spending all that money to send a whale back to where it was captured? To Iceland, of all places. It's criminal."

"You were talking about how Chuck came to write this story."

"Oh, sorry. This was his first news story. The issue closed while I was in Portland for some medical tests. I've been getting dizzy."

"Look, Mr. Gates. I'm not here to hassle you. I know Chuck. I have reason to think he's deliberately trying to hurt me."

A puzzled look came over the old man's face.

"It's too long and complicated to get into here. Let's just say he doesn't like me very much."

"Wanda."

"Yes, Mr. Gates."

"Where is Chuck? Tell him to get his miserable body in here—pronto."

"He went to make his ad calls at about the time I escorted Mr. Martingale back to your office."

"Drat. Tell him to get his sorry ass in here when he returns."

"Yes, Mr. Gates."

I glanced at my watch. It was 11:30, and I needed to get going if I was to make my appointment with Nate Golden and the Germans at Simone's house.

"I don't want to prolong this. I didn't come here to make trouble for you. I can see you had no knowledge of what Chuck was doing. I'll admit I came in here with a lawsuit on my mind. I don't think that will be necessary if you'll just print a retraction. Check with the sheriff to verify that I'm not a suspect. Or the state police."

The old man looked very relieved. "What do you want me to say?"

I grabbed a pencil and pad from his desk and jotted down a few lines, then tore off the page and handed it to him. "Run something like this in a box in a prominent place."

"Page one, I promise."

He read it and nodded. "In over fifty years in this business, I've never had anything like this happen to me before. I'm very sorry. I thank you for your decency. I was just trying to help Bernice's boy."

"I'll deal with Chuck, Mr. Gates. For your sake and the safety of everything you've worked so hard to achieve," I waved my arm toward the newsroom behind me, "I don't think you can trust him."

F ive minutes later, I drove up to Simone's house where Nate Golden was waiting.

"Hi, Nate. Hope I didn't interrupt your lunch."

"No, I had a late breakfast."

"Good. Let me fill you in on things before we go in." We stood by my car and did not move toward the front door. "We'll be meeting with Rose Edwards, the housekeeper. And there will be Manfred—call him Fred—Bader, a German professor who seems to have an interest in Simone's affairs."

"What do you mean?"

"He's been asking Rose a lot of questions—too many questions, in my opinion. It seems strange that he'd be willing to drive over here from Corvallis just to help straighten up a room."

"You've got a suspicious and cunning mind, Tom," laughed Golden. "But you may be right about that."

"Oh, he's also bringing along a relative—a guy visiting from Germany, I guess. That's all I know. That's my fill-in for you."

"Fill-in? You're getting this police lingo down amazingly well, Tom. It may not be too late to make a midcareer change."

"No, thanks. One midlife crisis is enough. Let's go in and talk to Rose."

The housekeeper opened the door just before I knocked.

"Hello, Rose. Meet Nate Golden of the Oregon State Police."

She took his hand and studied his face. "I think I saw you with madame one day out here in the driveway."

"I don't think so. I've never been here that I recall." Golden turned red, then shook her hand and bowed slightly. Rose stepped aside and ushered us in.

"Let's go back into the kitchen. I've got brunch ready to serve."

"What about Bader and his friend?"

"He called and won't be here until 1:30 or so. Car trouble."

"Good. That will give us time to look the study over. Sound like a plan, Nate?"

I was sure he wanted to get right into his investigation, but I didn't want to ruin Rose's good meal. She motioned us to the table and served plates of scrambled eggs, fried potatoes, and scones in front of us, followed by hot coffee. I learned a long time ago that a bachelor should never pass up the chance to eat a home-cooked meal prepared by a good cook.

As we ate, Rose sat down and repeated her story about the break-in, and then turned to me.

"Have you had any luck finding Adam? Is it all right to talk about it?" She glanced nervously at Golden.

"Nate's a friend," I said. "You can speak freely in front of him. I don't know any more than I did when we spoke earlier."

Rose started sobbing and put her head on the table. Golden looked alarmed, as I walked around the table to put my arm around her.

"He is a good boy. He wouldn't do anything to hurt anyone," she said.

"Take it easy, Rose. We'll find him."

"Boy. Great food. Thanks very much, Mrs. Edwards," Golden said, embarrassed by the sudden burst of emotion.

"I think it's time to take a look at the study," I said. "I'm anxious for Officer Golden's discerning eye to see what the rest of us have missed."

We all went back through the foyer and down the steps into the living room to the study where Rose selected a key from several on a ring in her hand and unlocked the door. She stepped aside to allow us to enter. Golden went first and slowly looked around the room. Nothing had been touched since the day before.

"I'll still go over things carefully—or get a team to come in," he said. "Now, what was on the computer?"

I sat down and turned on the machine. The computer purred into life and, in a few minutes all that appeared on the screen were the usual floating gobs of color familiar to computer users everywhere.

"I don't get it," I said. "This is just the usual stuff."

Golden stepped closer, as I frantically punched keys and then turned the computer off and on again, and waited. Still only colored gobs.

"You sure you know what you're doing, Tom?" he asked.

"That Nazi stuff was on the screen saver, Nate, so it should come up," I replied. "Rose, are you sure no one came in here, I mean since yesterday when you found all of this."

"No, sir. No one."

"And you didn't hear anything unusual?" Golden added.

"Only some cats, I think. Early this morning."

"Cats, you say?" Golden persisted.

Rose stepped into the room and sat down in a chair by the door. "A crash, like glass breaking, and then a tinny sound, like a garbage can lid rattling. We have some wild cats in the neighborhood."

Golden walked over to the tall windows on the west wall of the room and looked out. He then dropped to his knees to examine the floor in front of the window.

"Ouch." His finger was bleeding, and he carefully removed a long, narrow shard of glass. "This little devil was lurking in the carpet."

He held the piece up between the thumb and forefinger of his other hand, then put it in a plastic evidence bag he pulled out of his pocket. He then pressed a handkerchief tightly against the cut.

"Bleeding much?" I asked.

"I'll only lose a quart or two," he laughed.

Golden then returned to the window and started pushing on the panes with his good hand. Stained-glass scenes alternated with clear panes. He began at waist level, then worked his way down.

"Here, I thought so."

A colorful lighthouse dropped into his hands without breaking. He held it up for me to see, then carefully placed it on a nearby sofa pillow.

"Somebody did a very clean job of removing this old pane, opening the window lock, getting in, then replacing it as he left. Expert work," he said, as he opened the window and looked out.

"Nothing much here that I can see."

He stepped out gingerly, testing whether he could keep his balance on the narrow strip of land bordering the cliff over the sea.

"Careful, Nate."

"Just call the coroner when I fall." In a few minutes he was down on his hands and knees. "Just what I hoped," he said.

"What's there?"

"Window glazing. Whoever broke in reset the glass when they left, like I said, and dropped some in the process."

"But in the dark, Nate?" I turned toward Rose, still sitting patiently next to the door. "When did you hear the noise?"

"Three or four this morning."

"Three or four this morning, Nate," I said, sticking my head out the window. "It was pretty dark then." But Nate had spotted something else. He stepped back into room, smiling broadly. There in his hand was a tiny flashlight.

14

A few minutes later, we were all back at the kitchen table, cups of steaming coffee in front of us.

"So'd this guy hold that flashlight in his mouth while he worked?" I asked.

"That's a pretty good guess, Tom. Then maybe he dropped it in his scramble to get away," Golden said.

"Makes perfect sense to me."

"Anything else in that room somebody would want, Mrs. Edwards?" Golden asked Rose.

"I didn't know much about what madame did in there, but I know she spent a lot of time working on her memoirs."

"Yes, she gave me some pages to read," I said. "She hinted at showing me more, but I'm not sure how much."

"What was it about, Tom?" Nate asked.

"The story of her work in the French Resistance during the war. She helped get American and British pilots out of Paris and then worked with others in her home village. Some pretty scary stuff happened to her. She was a heroine in her own way. But was there more?"

We both looked at Rose, who shrugged her shoulders. "I just can't say."

"Let's crank up the computer and see if we . . ." said Nate, just as the doorbell rang.

"That's probably Fred Bader," I said, as Rose went to answer the door. "He's that German professor I mentioned."

Golden raised an eyebrow. "Refresh my memory. Why is he coming here today?"

"To help clean up the study, according to what he told Rose. I don't believe that for a minute. That's why I wanted you to be here."

"Here's Mr. Martindale and his friend," Rose said as she showed Fred Bader and another man into the kitchen. If he was startled to see an Oregon State Police officer sitting at the table, he didn't let on. He smiled as we both stood and he shook my hand.

"Tom. So good to see you again," he said.

"Great to see you, Fred, even under such sad circumstances. This is my friend Nate Golden of the Oregon State Police," I said.

The two shook hands.

"Manfred. Introduce me to your friends," said the man with Fred.

"Oh, yes, of course. Gentlemen, please allow me to present my cousin Count Fritz von Brandenberg, who is visiting me from Germany."

Bader's cousin, a tall, thin man with fine features and a regal bearing to match his title, stepped forward, bowed slightly, and shook, first my hand and then Golden's. "My pleasure to meet two of Manfred's more illustrious friends," he said in a heavy German accent. Golden looked amused, but said nothing.

"Here we are." Rose Edwards quietly placed two more cups of coffee on the table along with a platter of scones. She motioned for us to sit. The count quickly walked around and pulled out her chair.

"Why, thank you, sir," she said.

The count sat across the table and looked directly at me with a pair of penetrating green eyes. They were like lasers, as Rose had said.

"A terrible thing about Simone," I said, managing to avert my eyes. "A great loss for everyone."

"Yes, yes. She was like an older sister to me," Bader said sadly, but with no emotion showing on his face. The room grew quiet for a few moments.

"Tom tells me you expressed some interest in looking over Ms. Godard's things," Golden said to Bader, bringing the silence to an end. "Just exactly what were you expecting to find?"

"Officer Golden, I don't know that I like the tone of your question," answered Bader, glaring. The count quickly placed his hand on his cousin's arm. "Sorry. I'm just very upset over Simone's death. I get upset sitting here among all her things." Now Bader looked as if he might cry. Either he was the world's greatest actor or he genuinely cared for our mutual friend, I thought. I couldn't decide.

"I just find it odd, that's all," said Golden. If he was playing "bad cop," was I to be the "good cop"? I'd wait and see.

"We were over here anyway," said Bader. "My cousin is visiting Oregon for the first time, and I wanted him to see our glorious coast, that's all. I'm also looking for a house to lease for a month or so."

"Well, great," I interjected, trying to lighten the tone of things, but sounding like a member of the chamber of commerce in the process. "There's lots to see, and you'll love living here."

"And I suggest that if you and your cousin are ready to get on with your tour, we won't keep you," added Golden.

Bader glanced at the count, me, and then at Rose. "I thought you needed my help in cleaning up Simone's study," he said to Rose.

"That room is part of a crime scene," Golden said, before Rose could answer. "It is part of my investigation into Simone Godard's death."

"But I thought she died of natural causes," Bader sputtered.

"We are not yet sure how she died, Mr. Bader. But while we are on the subject of her study, would you happen to know anything about some Nazi emblems left on her computer?"

Von Brandenberg rose from the table. "Manfred. You don't have to take such verbal abuse from this Jew . . . this policeman."

Golden was instantly on his feet. "I'm going to ignore that," he said. "In your country, people like me weren't allowed to be policemen or much of anything else not all that long ago."

"How dare you speak about my country in such a manner," shouted von Brandenberg. "I won't have it."

Bader and I stepped in. He took the count's arm and eased him back into his chair.

"Nate. This is getting a little heavy, don't you think?" I asked quietly.

He shrugged his shoulders and remained standing.

"I need to know if Mr. Bader knows anything about the vandalism."

"I have no idea what you are talking about, sergeant," said Bader. "I've never been in that room."

"So, if we take fingerprints off anything there, we wouldn't find yours or your cousin's."

"That is what I am saying, sergeant," answered the German steadily.

"Okay, great," said Golden. "But why do you have any interest at all?"

"Merely to help, I can assure you, sergeant," said Bader. "And I hoped to locate a book of mine Simone borrowed several months ago."

"Now, we're getting somewhere," said Golden. "I suppose you were just going to take it—right out of a murder scene."

"I had no idea that her study had become—in your words—a murder scene," said Bader, holding his own. "For me, it was a lovely room with views of the sea where Simone Godard spent . . ."

"If you haven't been in the room," said Golden, "how did you know it overlooked the sea?

"I . . . remember her . . . I . . ." Bader was stumbling now.

The count quickly stood, took hold of his cousin's arm, and headed toward the door.

"Go ahead and go," said Golden in reply, "but don't leave the state, Mr. Bader. And you, too, Count von Brandenberg. We'll need to know where you are."

We three just stared at one another until the front door slammed.

"Don't you think you overreacted a bit, Nate?" I said. "I mean, I agree with your suspicions, but I wonder . . . well . . . are you going to get into trouble over this? I mean, Bader might raise a stink, and if he does, how will it affect your career?"

"I don't know about that," Golden replied, shaking his head. "I've met people like the count before. They treat Jews like it was Germany in 1936. It makes me crazy. I guess it affects my judgment. I apologize to both of you."

He glanced at me, then turned to face Rose, a sad smile on his face.

"Don't worry, Mr. Golden," she said softly. "I understand."

"So do I, Nate," I added. "I just don't want you to get into trouble."

"I think we need a more thorough search of the study," Golden said. "I need to make a call."

Rose pointed to a wall phone near the stove. He walked over and punched in a number.

"He'll get the investigation moving," I said, keeping my voice low. "I don't have much to report about Adam, as I've said. I was inside his room at the cemetery, but haven't looked anywhere else. You called, and I got sidetracked at the newspaper office." I looked over to make sure I wasn't interfering with Nate's call, and I wanted to make sure he wasn't listening to me.

"I found a key in his desk," I continued. "Is it for a shack at the quarry?"

She nodded, just as Nate was hanging up.

"That's done," said Golden, as he came over to the table. "Did I miss anything?" he laughed.

"We didn't want to distract you," I said, "so we were whispering."

I lied easily these days, blaming this transgression on the fact that it was for the greater good. Adam Edwards would not make a very good arrestee. Nate Golden was humane, but Sheriff Kutler wasn't. And he would be in Kutler's jail. I needed to keep my search to myself for now.

"Well, I've got a team coming within the hour."

I got up and looked at my watch. "It's almost 3:30, and I've got some errands to run." I turned to Golden and shook his hand. "Thanks for getting involved in this. I really appreciate your help."

"It's my job, Tom. I'll walk you out. I need to get a notebook out of my car." Golden looked drained—his face pale, deep circles under his eyes.

"Look, Nate," I said, when we got outside. "I want to be your friend. You were quite heated in there. Is there anything I can help you with?"

He didn't say anything for a few moments, and when he did his voice was so low I could barely hear him. "A lot of my family died at Treblinka. My grandfather survived and came to this country. I was close to him when I was growing up in Brooklyn. He told me what happened to the family. Over and over, he kept saying, 'Nate, this can never be allowed to happen again.' I was never permitted to forget what had gone on." His eyes filled with tears.

"I know, I know," I said, thinking how ironic it was that Simone had written her memoir on this same period of history.

"When I heard about the Nazi stuff on the computer and talked to Bader and his cousin, all my childhood memories came back. If Simone Godard was killed because of something in that writing she gave you, it means the killing is still going on—all these years later." Golden stared into space, his face hardening.

"It means something else, too," he said after a long pause. "That kind of evil must be stopped."

N ate insisted on reading Simone's memoir, and I agreed to show it to him the next day. Meanwhile, I spent the rest of the afternoon puttering around my house. Although I was anxious to continue my search for Adam Edwards at the rock quarry, I couldn't risk doing it in daylight. Maybe tonight, if I could pry myself loose from Connie Wright. I wasn't looking forward to her come-hither looks and sexual innuendoes, but I needed the rest of Simone's manuscript. I would put up with anything—even jingling bracelets and heaving breasts—to get it.

I left my house about 6:30. The Miroco community has one of the most spectacular views on the Oregon coast, and the homes cling to a solid rock table high above the ocean. This makes the area stable and not prone to the erosion that plagues some ocean communities. But it bears the brunt of winter storms because there is nothing to shield it from their fury.

The sunset was all reds and yellows that were shimmering on the placid sea as I turned off U.S. Highway 101 and doubled back along the side road across a bridge and into Miroco itself. Most of the house numbers were obscured by plants or missing entirely, and I missed Connie's house the first time past. As I turned around, I noticed a white car dart out of a driveway about half a block up on the ocean side of the street. I got a good look at it because the driver paused and seemed to stare directly at me before he sped away. The car—an older Honda four-door—looked vaguely familiar.

The driveway he had exited belonged to the very house I was looking for—#55. The numbers were partially hidden by ivy clinging to the bricks. Suddenly I had a funny feeling in my stomach, as I turned in and eased my car down the steep driveway.

Connie's house was as imposing as Simone's: a slate gray, saltbox style with dormer windows set off by a cedar shingle roof. A long porch led from the driveway to the front door. I rang the bell and waited.

After a moment or so, I peered through the stained-glass window at the side of the door—whales breaching above a turbulent sea—but I could barely see through the few open spots into the house. I could make out a wide hall leading to a doorway that opened into a large room. I tried the door and found it unlocked, so I stepped inside onto an expensive oak plank floor.

"Connie? It's Tom Martindale. I'm early."

Nothing.

"Connie, I'm coming in."

I walked slowly down the hall to the sun-drenched room at the end. I could hear soft music playing—elevator music. I could just imagine Connie ordering *Music for Lovers* or *Music to Eat Dinner By* from one of those ads on cable TV.

"Strangers in the Night" was just ending as I entered the beautifully appointed room—all richly upholstered sofas and chairs and expensive wooden tables holding massive glass vases filled with flowers.

"Connie. Are you in here?"

I turned toward the doorway to the dining room as "Lara's Theme" from *Dr. Zhigavo* started playing.

Connie Wright was lying on her back near the door to the kitchen, a tray of food spilled over her colorful silk caftan.

I called Nate Golden, then sat down in the living room. My shock at finding Connie's body was slowly giving way to curiosity mixed with fear. I'd better make sure I'm alone, I thought.

As I crept up the stairway to the second floor, I picked up a heavy wooden cane I found in a rack on the landing, just in case I needed a weapon. The stairs were heavily carpeted, but they squeaked after every step I took. I paused each time, straining to hear any sign that someone might still be lurking in the rooms above.

Three closed doors lined the upstairs hall. With my heart pounding, I opened the first one: a guest room full of chintz and big roses and teddy bears. The next door was slightly ajar, and I could hear the slow drip of water. A nudge on the door revealed the guest bathroom. My careful opening of the third door revealed more chintz, ruffles, and teddy bears. I slowly entered with the cane raised in front of me. As I moved to the window, the bears' glass eyes seemed to follow me—it was an eerie feeling.

A fluttering sound stopped me cold. My eyes fell on a tall, shrouded object next to the canopied bed. I gently lifted the covering and found myself staring into the unblinking eyes of the largest parrot I had ever seen.

"Connie's good boy," he said, moving his head to one side.

Although I could always have lively conversations with dogs and cats, I couldn't bring myself to say anything to this plumed creature. I turned and quickly got the hell out of there, feeling a small trickle of sweat run down my spine. A shudder engulfed me as I closed the door and bounded down the stairs.

At that moment, Nate Golden came in the front door, followed by several other officers and two technicians wearing coveralls.

"God, Nate. I'm glad to see you."

"I got here as soon as I could," he answered. "Where's the body?"

"Is that the weapon you used to kill Ms. Wright, professor? I think you'd better drop it right now." I looked down at the heavy wooden cane clutched in my hand and handed it to Nate as Sheriff Kutler pushed into the room. "Shall I read him his rights, Sergeant Golden, or will you?"

"Right, sheriff," I said, taking the offensive. "I'm going to kill someone, call the police, then ransack her house while I wait for you to get here to arrest me. That makes a lot of sense. I thought whoever killed Connie might still be around, so I went upstairs to look."

"And disturb the crime scene," said Kutler, adding another accusation to his list.

"Find anyone, Tom?" asked Golden, ignoring the sheriff.

"Only a parrot who kept said he was Connie's good boy."

"And here I thought *you* were about to become Connie's good boy," hissed Kutler. "How is it that these older babes don't last long once you start hanging around them, professor?"

"Sheriff, why don't you go blow up a whale or something?"

Kutler's face reddened, as he grabbed me by the shirt.

"Whoa, sheriff," said Golden, as he pulled him off. "Take it easy."

Kutler stepped back, shaking himself loose. Without saying another word, he turned and stomped out the door, his deputies falling in behind him.

"Wasn't that a great show of police restraint?" I said, sitting down on the stairs.

"I don't see why you say stuff like that to set him off, Tom," said Golden. "You know how that gets under his skin."

"It's my superior intellect, Nate," I laughed. "I got the last laugh before, and it galls him."

"He's not someone you should piss off, Tom. Don't you get it?"

I shrugged, thinking Nate was probably right, and led him to Connie Wright's body. After the technicians started their work, Nate and I returned to the hall.

"You may not think he's smart, but he's got a badge and a gun and the legal authority to haul your academic ass into jail. I can't always be around to come to your rescue," he said.

I made a mental note to behave around Kutler. I'd have to save my wise-ass, smart-mouth side for the classroom.

"Did you find anything upstairs?" he asked.

"I wasn't looking, really. I honestly thought someone might still be in the house. That's why I grabbed the cane."

"Let's go up and see what we find," Golden said.

He quickly checked the guest room and bathroom, but only glanced around. Then we headed for the master bedroom. He walked slowly around, looking but not touching.

"Ms. Wright was really a neat freak," he said. "Let's check the closet."

Just then he bumped into the shrouded cage.

"Connie's good boy. Connie's good boy."

"Jesus." Golden shouted, jumping back, his hand instinctively going to his revolver.

"The parrot. Remember?"

"Yeah, yeah. I forgot."

I followed him into the large, walk-in closet. Connie Wright apparently liked clothes because the racks were filled. From silk caftans to tweed suits and fur coats to negligees, she had put a lot of her money into what she wore. One section of shelves held probably a hundred sweaters. Another long rack would have made Imelda Marcos proud: at least eighty pairs of shoes, sandals, and slippers.

Everything was neat and in order, but then we both spotted one thing out of place: a cordless drill with a broken bit lying on a roughed-up area of carpet at the far end.

"Looks like our murderer was doing some unauthorized home maintenance," said Golden, getting down on his knees.

He was careful not to touch the handle as he moved the drill out of the way. He reached over and pulled up the edge of the rug, revealing the round door of a small safe imbedded in the floor.

"Looks like our guy knew what he was looking for."

He bent closer.

"This baby's pretty firm. Look at this."

I got down on my knees.

"He drilled around the handle, the hinges, even the combination tumbler. All to no avail," said Golden. "Either he gave up or he heard you and got the hell out of here."

"Simone's papers."

"What?"

"A package of papers Simone left for me. That's the reason I came here tonight."

"Why would anybody want to steal them?"

"For a name maybe."

"Of someone living around here? With a link to World War II? Nazis in Depoe Bay? That seems pretty much of a stretch, Tom. Even . . ."

"Even for me?" I laughed. "That's just what Angela Pride always says about the stuff I do."

"Sorry," Golden replied. "I guess I don't know you well enough to say something like that."

"Be my guest," I said, raising my hands in mock resignation.

"We've got to get this open," Golden said. Speaking into the tiny microphone of a two-way radio strapped to his shoulder, he said, "Paul. Can you come up here?" Then, as an aside to me, "We've got this tech who's good with safes."

"Yes, boss?" said a voice behind us, as a young guy with a spiked crew cut and one of those mustache and goatee combinations every other man is now wearing to look cool and mysterious came into the room. He was wearing blue coveralls with an Oregon State Police patch on one side and Rodino on the other.

"Paul Rodino, meet Tom Martindale."

We shook hands.

"See if you can work your magic fingers on this safe."

Rodino got down on all fours and placed his ear to the dial as he slowly turned it.

"Sounds like a #14 Mastersafe," he said. "Shouldn't be too hard." He then pulled a tool out of his pocket that had a magnet on one end, hunched over the tumbler, and kept turning the dial, maneuvering the tool back and forth. Before long, there was a clicking sound and then a slight squeak as the door opened.

"Paul, you're a genius." Golden said. "I'm going to have to get you a promotion."

"How about Tech I?" said Rodino, a smile on his face.

"Yeah, Tech I."

"Wow," the technician said, as he got out of our way.

"Thanks a lot, Paul," Golden said, shaking his hand. "We'll take it from here. I'll let you get back to your work downstairs. We need to get that body out of the house as soon as possible."

"You've got one happy techie there, Nate," I laughed, as Rodino left.

Golden nodded, as he directed his attention to the safe.

"Do you need a court order or something to get in there?" I asked.

"This is part of an ongoing murder investigation," he answered. "The drill, the holes—all of this was done by the murderer, I expect. I'll take responsibility."

Golden began to pull things out. "Looks like jewelry," he said, as he laid a long velvet bag on the floor next to me.

"Maybe insurance policies and stocks and bonds in this," he said, glancing inside a brown legal folder.

"Look. This must be what our perp was after." He pulled out a manila envelope about a half-inch thick with my name written on the outside in Simone's unmistakable calligraphy-like handwriting.

"Monsieur Tom," read the inscription. Her pet name for me. A wave of sadness overcame me, and my eyes filled with tears as Golden handed me the parcel.

"Easy, Tom. Let's go out into the bedroom and sit down."

Quickly taking a seat, I tore open the sealed flap and pulled out the thick sheaf of papers. I hurriedly thumbed through them until the truth sunk in: the pages were completely blank.

I was stunned.

"That was one smart lady," said Golden, shaking his head.

"She was one step ahead of whoever is after this stuff."

I had to agree, as I kept fanning the pages, hoping to find some clue. I finally spotted what I was looking for: a photo-copy of a photo of a World War II pilot, dressed in a leather jacket and flight cap.

"Here, look at this," I shouted to Golden, who had gone back into the closet.

"What'd you find?" he asked, appearing in the doorway.

"A copy of a photo," I answered, holding it up.

"So, who is this guy? Her boyfriend, her father, who?"

"It isn't who he is that matters, it's what he stands for."

"Okay. I'm listening."

"One of the events in Simone's memoir is her time as a courier for the French Resistance in Paris during the German occupation," I explained. "Her main job was to meet American and British pilots who had crashed behind enemy lines, but not been captured."

"Meet them how?"

"Usually in the Metro—the subway. Someone else would bring a pilot to her, they would act like lovers, and she would guide the guy onto the correct train and ride with him to meet the next person. Kind of like the underground railroad that helped slaves escape the South before the Civil War. She did this for over a year."

"So, you say the guy in the photo stands for something? What do you mean?"

"Hide in plain sight."

"I'm not sure I follow."

"The French Resistance was successful in getting hundreds of pilots out of France because they led them around right under the noses of the Germans. I think Simone is telling me the same thing. The rest of her memoir is sitting somewhere so visible no one would ever suspect."

"But where?"

"That's what we've got to figure out."

Golden sat down, and we both stared into space for a few moments.

"What could be so damaging in this stuff anyway?" he asked, breaking the silence.

"I'm assuming she wrote about someone who is still living," I said.

"And that someone wants to prevent disclosure," he answered.

"It's got to be the Germans."

"Bader and his cousin?"

"Yeah, I guess."

"Look Tom, you can't go around accusing people of murder because you think there's some Nazi link. Even I wouldn't want to go that far."

"Well, somebody's guilty, and it might be the person in a car I saw speed off when I drove up."

"Why didn't you mention it before? What kind of car?"

I thought for a moment.

"Seemed like an older Honda, white."

"You didn't see a license number, I suppose?"

"No. There wasn't any reason to."

Golden stood up and smoothed out his uniform.

"I've got to get back downstairs. You'd better come with me."

We headed down the stairs, Golden leading the way. The other state police officers and the technicians were still working in the kitchen and dining room. As Golden walked into the living room, one of his co-workers whispered something to him and he nodded.

"They're going to take her body out now, Tom. Let's go outside."

"It's good to get some fresh air," I said, as we stood by my car. "Do you want me to write out a statement?"

"Yes, I do," he answered, "for the record."

"I'll do it first thing in the morning. Right now I'm going to concentrate on the hide-in-plain-sight scenario. I'll figure it out, Nate."

"Figure it out carefully, Tom. We both know that Sheriff Kutler loves to come up with reasons to arrest you."

"I know, I know. Sometimes he moves pretty fast—for a fat man."

Golden wrote something down on the back of his business card and handed it to me.

"My pager number. I only give it out for highly sensitive cases. You'll always be able to reach me on it."

"I certainly qualify, then. I'm the most highly sensitive case I know."

We both laughed, then I got into the car and returned Golden's wave as I drove down the street and out of Miroco, heading onto the intersecting road and across the short bridge. At the stop sign, I looked to my left before entering Highway 101. A white Honda sedan was parked in a small wayside where people stopped to watch the ocean. Suddenly, the driver pulled directly in my path and rolled down the window.

"How'd you like that little story?" Chuck Gates shouted.

I jumped out and headed for him. Gates was laughing, but his face darkened as I approached.

"How's it feel to have your life hung out to dry, Mr. High and Mighty Professor?" he hissed.

"Look, Chuck . . ."

"Mr. Gates to you, prick."

"I know you think I ruined your life."

"Two years, five months, and fifteen days to be exact."

"Whatever. I'm afraid you can't work in a public institution and act like . . ."

"Afraid? You don't know the meaning of the word. Your pals Simone and Connie didn't." He was smirking now, his eyes flashing.

"You sick bastard," I shouted, lunging at him through the open window. But Gates gunned the engine and his car lurched forward, barely missing my feet before I jumped out of the way.

I ran to my car and sped onto the highway, hoping Gates was still in sight. I tried Golden's pager number on my cell phone, but none of my calls went through.

Just then, I spotted Gates's car parked on the shoulder a half-mile ahead. He pulled out when he saw me, speeding up, then slowing down, making sure I was behind him. He wanted me to follow him, but why?

I t took Gates fifteen minutes to reach the Yaquina Bay Bridge.

Every few minutes I punched in Golden's pager number on my cell phone, but still had no success reaching him. I almost hoped to run across a sheriff's cruiser, but the streets of Newport were deserted. Where was Art Kutler when I needed him? I dismissed that thought as soon as it entered my head. The sheriff would arrest me for following Gates too closely or concoct a similarly ridiculous excuse to haul me in.

I followed Gates across the bridge and into the series of right turns that would take us to the Oregon Coast Aquarium. I couldn't figure out why he was headed there, except that it would be an ideal place to tie up a last loose end by killing me.

Foolishly, perhaps, I didn't think it would come to that. I had to find out what Gates knew about Simone's murder, no matter what the danger.

We drove into the aquarium grounds and Gates headed down a service road on one side of the main building. He had obviously learned the layout of the place when he wrote the newspaper stories. I decided to park in the main lot and take my chances on foot.

When I reached the end of the road, Gates's car was parked next to the loading dock. I walked slowly around to the driver's side and called his name. No response. The car was empty.

I turned to my right at the sound of a metal door moving slightly in the gentle breeze. Gates couldn't have made his intention to have me follow him any clearer if he had stood in the opening and beckoned me in.

I walked through the door and into a long passageway that led to a bright light at the other end. I moved forward slowly and soon found myself standing above a large tank, its water shimmering in the illumination from the floodlights around the perimeter. I knew from seeing all the film footage on television that this had been, until recently, the home of Keiko. The killer whale had been rescued from an amusement park in Mexico City and brought here to the aquarium for rehabilitation and preparation for release back into the waters of Iceland where he had been captured twenty years before.

The return to Iceland had been controversial because Keiko was so used to being fed by humans that he couldn't catch live fish on his own. Aquarium officials had opposed his release and a public feud had erupted between them and Keiko's owners. After many press releases and heated exchanges between the two sides, Keiko had been transported to a new floating pen in a fjord in Iceland a few months ago.

Aquarium officials planned to replace the whale with a new sea exhibit that would include octopus, sharks, and various rare fish species. Visitors would be able to walk under the water in a Plexiglas tunnel, but that new area was many months away from opening. The empty tank made me feel sad and lonely, as I walked around it, trying to spot the underwater windows where the whale and his adoring public had delighted one another for several years.

Where was Gates?

"Gates," I shouted. "I want to talk to you. Don't let your feelings about me cause you to do anything stupid."

At first, my words were all that pierced the balmy night air. The tank and adjacent deck were quiet except for the sound of the water lapping against the side. Soon, however, I heard a bubbling sound at the far end, as if the jets of a hot tub had been turned on. I walked toward the sound on the other side. Reaching it, I realized it was coming from the orca's medical area, a smaller pool where he would swim in for medical tests.

"Gates," I tried again, moving through the opening into the medical area. "Let's cut out this cat and mouse game, shall we?"

I didn't see him move out of the shadows and shove me into the water. I plunged to the bottom, but soon surfaced in the center of the small pool.

"Make that shark and prey," he yelled, "shall we, professor?"

At that point, a sudden movement caught my eye, and I turned my head to see a large shark swim by in the main tank. I paddled to the side, but Gates was there before me, jabbing at me with a long pole that had a lethal-looking hook on the end.

"Not so fast, Martindale. I don't want you to miss the aquarium's newest attraction—a tiger shark. He'd love to meet you. I just know it."

Gates started laughing, initial low chuckles turning into a high-pitched manic cackle. Then, he repeatedly lunged at me with the hook, probably as much to keep me in the pool as to wound or kill me—that honor he was reserving for my snaggle-toothed friend in the other tank.

I had done enough reading and seen enough documentaries on The Discovery Channel to know that sharks usually attacked humans when they mistook them for seals—their natural prey—or were attracted by blood in the water. I kicked off my shoes and paddled over to the entrance of the medical pool where the gates were closed. If I could get over them, maybe I could escape to the outside area and away from him.

As I reached the opening, it occurred to me that Gates might have wired the fence. I knew I would be fried to a crisp if I grabbed the steel mesh of the chain link fence while I was in the water. I probed tentatively with my wallet. Sparks flew as the electricity burned a hole in the leather.

"Didn't mean to shock you, old friend," he shouted from behind, amid more laughter.

Maybe he meant to scare me, I thought, grateful, at least, that these doors were closed. The shark must have been swimming elsewhere in the large tank because I couldn't see him. I was determined to keep calm and be as unseal-like as possible while I figured out what to do. I decided to try reason again and swam back to where Gates was standing.

"Have I got your attention, pal?" he said.

"You do, Chuck."

"Mr. Gates to you."

"Mr. Gates. Sorry, I forgot. Why not let me out of here and we'll talk."

"About what? How you cost me my job at the U of O, a job I loved and was good at. You dug up that crap from my past that said I was a loony, and it got me fired."

He had the scenario slightly wrong, but this was no time to quibble. He had gotten himself fired from the marketing job at the University of Oregon after obsessing on an ad campaign I was running to recruit students to my college. He had broken into my office on campus to steal a script, and even disrupted filming on campus. That is what had gotten him fired. But I wasn't about to mention it now.

"Look, Gates. Won't you accept my apology? I admit I over-reacted then. Your ad campaign was so much better than mine, I had to stop you somehow."

If reason didn't work, perhaps a little bullshit would. As I spoke, I turned my head and noticed the shark floating quietly in the water just outside the entrance, its one dead eye seemingly fixed on me.

"Now we're getting somewhere," said Gates, suddenly susceptible to my flattery. "Hearing the truth really makes me feel better."

Gates's change of tone made me think he was going to be reasonable after all. He'd let me out of the water, and we could talk about all of this in a civil way. I would be on my way without saying a thing about any murders.

But just then, he poured a dark brown substance into the water as the metal gates slid open.

"Close, but no cigar," said Gates, as the shark darted through the opening, straight toward me and the blood around me.

I tucked my legs and one arm into as tight a ball as I could, so that nothing would be dangling. With the other arm, I eased myself along the side of the pool away from Gates and toward a small door just above the water line. It probably led to a service area that would be big enough to hold me, if I could get the door open.

Gates was fixated on the shark, which had begun making narrowing circles around the tank. He didn't notice me move out of the light and into the shadow that hid the door. I alternately watched both him and the shark as I reached the door.

"Here sharky, sharky," he yelled, as he poured in more blood. The words came out in a sing-song manner like a child taunting playmates. Although he was laughing, he sounded desperate.

Just then, Gates realized he couldn't see me. "Martindale. Where are you?"

I was away from the bloody water, concentrating on opening the door. The shark was still circling, so I tried to keep the water as placid as possible.

"Martindale. Did you meet our toothy friend already? Is that why you're not talking? What a shame. I'll miss you." Gates had stepped over the line that separates the sane from the insane.

The door had a small ring at the top, but it didn't yield at my first tug. It had probably been designed to be opened from the inside. I tried again, only to draw blood as the wire cut into my finger. That I didn't need.

The shark was getting curious about this ball-like creature capable of occasional bursts of energy. It swam nearer with each pass. At one point, I could feel motion as it sped by. A moment later, I looked up in time to catch its eye looking at me.

As I got into the rhythm of its laps around the pool, I realized they were only about a minute or so apart. Even though it was swimming out into the main tank, the shark wasn't staying there very long before returning to me. I confined my efforts to open the door to times when the shark was swimming away from me.

Another few minutes or so passed. It seemed like hours as I frantically clawed at the door. Despite the cold water, I felt hot all over as if pins were sticking into me. Does fear do that to you? Why had I followed Gates here at all? Why do I constantly get myself into messes that are impossible to get out of?

Finally, the door yielded slightly. Its hinges were at the bottom. If I forced it open wide enough, I could slide into what

I hoped would be a tunnel or a hall. Hell, I would even settle for a cupboard.

The door budged a bit more as I heard splashing behind me. I had abandoned any effort to remain in a ball and was using both hands to get the door open. I turned to see three bloody fish floating right in front of me. Gates had thrown them in, redoubling his efforts to get the shark to include me in its meal plan.

The creature was ready to play its role. On cue, it came straight for the fish, barely missing my left leg as it gobbled them up with the precision of a combine cutting wheat in a field. It passed me closely, this time in the opposite direction. I noticed a deep scar running above and below one eye. Then, I remembered what I had read about plans for the tank in this post-Keiko era. Aquarium officials intended to rehabilitate injured marine creatures here. This was their first patient: a shark with one blind eye. But it still had that keen sense of smell and hearing that I remembered reading about. The more I thought about it, the more I decided my chances of escaping harm were probably less than fifty percent.

At that point, more adrenaline kicked in, and I made a last desperate pull on the ring. This time the door opened wide enough for me to dive in, head first. I landed face down in a pile of fish. All I needed: all those dead eyes staring at me.

I scrambled around and sat up to close the door. The shark hurled itself at my outstretched hand, cutting a deep gash. The fish smell and concern about losing me as a meal were impelling it onward; it was trying to come in after me.

I grabbed a metal bucket and pushed at its snout; it yielded, slipping backward. I heard a splash and, later, the occasional whoosh its body made as it sped by. I slammed the door and sat down to catch my breath. One monster down, one to go.

In the dim light, I could see blood running down my hand. I pulled off a sock and made a tourniquet. The wound wasn't as deep as I feared, and the bleeding stopped immediately. I'd need stitches, but I could function well enough to get away.

I crept along the metal floor, which inclined slightly to another opening with no door. I pulled myself up and over the top with my good hand, swung my legs around, and dropped several feet to a cement floor. A number of freezers lined the walls. A long steel table sat in the center of the room.

At the other end, I eased a door open and looked out into a hall. The only sound came from the generators used to purify the water in the tank. I listened carefully before I stepped out and started running as fast as I could.

I soon made it to the area where millions of people had viewed the now departed Keiko through large windows. From there, I ran out into the courtyard, and to the doors of the main building. They were locked. I continued around to the holding tanks for the seals and otters. As I climbed over the wall behind their enclosures, I saw the comical little critters floating on their backs in the water, watching me intently.

"Fine for you to be cute and perky," I muttered to them. "I'm a mess."

I dropped to the ground on the outer perimeter of the aquarium and took off to where I had left my car. I had just unlocked and opened the door when headlights suddenly flashed in my face as a vehicle came out of the darkness. I dove in and felt my car shudder as the other vehicle rammed it. Gates was having another crack at me.

I shoved the key in the ignition, and the motor started on the first try. I hit first gear and barreled away. Gates's ancient heap would be no match for this baby. Even though it was wounded, my car easily outran his.

It was two in the morning when I finally walked through my front door. I had explained my wound to the attending physician in the emergency room as an accident I had while cleaning fish. I guess he believed my story because he said little as he sewed me up—five stitches worth—and sent me on my way. I had managed to get out of my wet shirt and pull on a clean sweatshirt I had in the car. I also found a pair of sneakers in the trunk. I still reeked of fish, but not as badly as before. And I was pleased to find that Gates had put only two small dents in my front bumper.

As I unlocked the front door, I saw that the light on my telephone answering machine was blinking.

listened to the phone message in the dark. "Professor Martindale, this is Stacy Thomas. We met at Simone's brunch the other day. I have those French poems she wanted you to read. Please call me so we can figure out how to get them to you. Bye for now."

As I wrote down her number, I realized I had just been handed the solution to the puzzle.

Thursday

Stacy Thomas had been introduced at the brunch as a former student who helped Simone with her research. I waited until ten the next morning to return her call, and she invited me over. A few minutes before eleven, I was knocking on the door of a small wooden house on one of the streets above Newport's old Bay Front section.

"Oh, hi," she said, as she opened the door and welcomed me inside. The house was old and smelled moldy, a common problem on the coast if buildings aren't well insulated. The floor creaked as I followed her down a long hall to a sun-drenched room at the end.

Stacy was pretty, and she knew it, not self-conscious at all in using her provocative clothing—a tank top and very short shorts—to attract attention.

"Move some of that stuff and sit down," she said, sprawling on a large beanbag chair and motioning toward a pile of newspapers, used food containers, and beer cans on an ancient overstuffed sofa that sagged in the middle. "I didn't have time to straighten up." The awkward angle of her chair thrust her legs toward me to reveal a lot more of her than I was comfortable looking at.

I sat down as soon as I cleared some space.

"What happened to you?" she asked, pointing to my bandaged hand.

"I got careless cleaning some fish. I was surprised to hear from you, Stacy."

"Forgot me so soon?" she said, thrusting her lower lip out as if I had hurt her feelings.

"How could anyone forget a great-looking girl like you," I replied, playing to her vanity, but beginning to wonder about her jealous boyfriend.

"Terrible about Simone," she said, changing the subject. "She was always good to me. But she was on my case a bit too much. She made me mad sometimes."

"On your case about what?"

"She said I was wasting my life here in Newport and not using my degree to start a career. She thought I had a natural ability with languages."

"That's rare," I added. "Few American kids do. Why don't you . . ."

"Make something of myself and get out of this dump?" she interrupted.

"Yeah, maybe."

"I'm not alone, you know. I live with my boyfriend, Joe George. You met him."

"Yes, I remember."

"He works at one of the canneries on the Bay Front, and he treats me like a queen. Doesn't want me to work. Just wants me to be waiting for him when he gets home." Her eyes turned dreamy. "We have the greatest sex," she continued. "It's unbelievable."

"I bet it is." This conversation was going down a road I wasn't very interested in taking. "You mentioned some poems Simone left you to give me?"

"Sorry. I got carried away thinking about my sex life. I guess other people aren't interested." She looked over at me and winked, tossing her head so abruptly her long hair seemed to move with a life of its own. She laughed, enjoying my discomfort.

At that moment, the front door flew open.

"Stacy, what the fuck?" Joe George was bursting out of some very scanty briefs. Maybe he had stripped off his smelly cannery clothes at the door, ready for a little roll in the beanbag chair before he showered.

"Hi, Joe. You remember Professor Martindale. From the brunch the other day? At Simone's?"

"A little home schooling?" he said, striding over to me. I pushed his arms away and sprang to my feet. He was bulky, but no taller than I was. We stood nose to nose.

"Look pal," I conjured up as much menace in my voice as I could. "I was invited over to pick up something that was left for me. I'd like to get it and be gone."

He seemed ready to pounce, but Stacy broke the tension.

"This is what you came for," she said, reaching under the beanbag chair and pulling out an envelope.

"Thanks. I'll be on my way," I said, as George backed away from me. I paused in the doorway. "Good luck with your career choice, Stacy."

She was laughing as I closed the front door behind me.

I resisted opening the envelope until I got home. I first made some coffee, then sat down to see what Simone had been so anxious for me to read.

"Tom," an attached note said, "I'm sorry for the cloak and dagger. I needed to keep this away from the wrong people. We'll laugh about this someday over drinks, I am certain. But right now I fear that what I wrote about in these pages will cause me harm. I need you to read this and act accordingly. Substitute the following for what I gave you earlier, beginning on page 8. S.G."

I put the note aside and with a heavy heart started reading.

Murders in Wartime
(Revised)

Even when they put us against the wall in the kitchen, I said again, "According to the terms of the armistice, you've got to have evidence." I was the very essence of cool and, probably, foolhardiness. Outwardly, I knew no fear, although my mouth was dry and I had to fight to keep my voice steady.

When the captain stepped over to me, I noticed at once something that nearly caused me to faint. Those cold, green eyes, cleft chin, and chiseled features—I had seen them all before. This was the same officer who had so impatiently presided over the checkpoint in the Paris Metro the year before.

I had no real worry that he would remember me—an anonymous face in a crowd of nobodies he was herding around.

"A bit cheeky are we, mademoiselle?*" he said, slightly amused at my effrontery.*

My mother glanced at me nervously, imploring me with her eyes to keep quiet. I, on the other hand, knew my law and the German penchant for order. "Evidence, Herr Kapitan,*" I said sweetly, shrugging my shoulders and raising my hands palms up in a gesture of doggedness. The officer paused and stroked his perfect chin. He stepped back and looked me over from head to toe.*

"Skillet," he said, laughing and mugging for the soldiers standing near the door. Skeleton. He was telling them that I was too thin. They were all smirking now.

He motioned for my mother to sit down at the table. Her eyes were wild with fear, but I pleaded with her in my return glance not to panic—just yet.

"Suche das haus," shouted the officer, gesturing toward the trap door which led to the cellar. One of the soldiers pulled it up and stepped carefully down the ladder. I could hear him stumbling over the boxes and farm tools until he found the light switch.

The officer remained standing in front of me—not blinking those horrible, all-seeing green eyes. I stared back as long as I could stand it, careful to keep my gaze somewhere between fear and hatred. He pulled a silver case out of his pocket.

"Mind if I smoke, madame*?" he addressed my mother as mistress of the house.*

She murmured her permission hesitantly, not looking directly at him. I could hear the soldiers searching below, occasionally breaking jars. Every time I had used the radio, I had returned it carefully to its hiding place in the well. The lid on the well was under some heavy barrels full of food. In a few minutes, the soldier's head appeared just above the floor line.

"Nichts, Herr Kapitan."

The officer took a drag on his cigarette. "Genug."

The search was over. He motioned for the soldier to come up and for the two other soldiers to take my mother outside. She started screaming, and one of the soldiers raised a hand ready to slap her. I stepped between them.

"Leave her alone. She's an old lady. Punish me, not my mother."

The soldier stopped his arm in midair and looked at the officer. He called him off. My mother was still weeping and barely able to walk as they dragged her outside.

I turned toward the officer and waited. He suddenly grabbed my arm, pulled me outside, and motioned toward the lighthouse at the base of the hill. Without hesitating, I walked slowly toward it, hoping my acquiescence would keep my mother from being hurt.

The lighthouse my father had tended for fifteen years was shimmering in the late morning sun, its white brick surface looking like a castle in a children's fairy tale. Up close, however, it resembled a medieval dungeon—with me, imagining what was about to happen, its only prisoner.

With my father away at his meeting, no one was around. Earlier in the war he had been forced to let his only assistant go. As a result, he had had to work long hours to ensure that the light never went out lest ships run aground on the rocky shoreline. He was only able to be away today because of the sunny, calm weather.

The captain motioned me inside. We both looked up at the dome which was barely visible because of the serpentine iron stairway. I placed one foot on the bottom step, but the captain touched my arm and shook his head.

"Nichts," he said, pointing to the trap door at the other end of the entry chamber. I walked to it, suddenly feeling numb all over. I pulled on the iron ring and the door creaked opened. A sudden surge of musty, cold air wafted up from below.

"Mademoiselle," he said, pointing downward.

We were about to descend the ladder I had once played on as a child. I hiked up my skirt and stepped into the hole. The captain followed me, and we were soon standing in the darkness of the small cellar. The only light shafted down from the opening above.

He pulled out a flashlight and soon found a large kerosene lantern and lit the wick with a match. The illumination, only slightly better than before, cast dark shadows on the brick walls as he carried the lantern to a table in the center of the room.

Then, he pointed to an old wooden chair, and I sat down. He then began to make a bed on the straw and pulled a tarp over it, making sure in his Germanic orderliness to smooth out any wrinkles. He motioned for me to lie down, and I did as I was told. I realized I had to submit to him to save my mother. Any resistance on my part would only make it worse for her.

The officer then started removing his clothes: his tunic and trousers, his shirt, his long underwear. I was too frightened to do anything but stare. Next, he began to unbutton my dress, and when it was open he pulled down my pantalets. By this time his penis was erect.

"This needn't be troubling to you, mademoiselle," *he whispered in my ear, as he got on top of me and pushed himself inside. "Just relax and enjoy it," he said, and moaned softly.*

I turned my head, trying not to gag from the smell of the damp, musty walls and the tarp. I tried to keep from shaking as he moved back and forth above me. I kept thinking of the spare radio and the ammunition I knew my father had stored down here. He had never told me precisely where, but I knew it was somewhere in the walls.

Somehow, those thoughts made it easier to cope with what was happening. With that radio I could have the last laugh and, eventually, rid the face of the earth of monsters like the Nazi officer on top of me.

With this single act, the captain had turned a childhood place of fun and adventure into a chamber of terror and degradation. When the ordeal was over, I was no longer a virgin.

Later, when we returned to the house, one of the soldiers guarding my mother rushed up to the officer and whispered in his ear. I only caught one word: "scheiben."

By this time, the other soldier had moved me over to my mother, who was standing at the front gate. She looked at me with sadness in her eyes and grabbed my hands, knowing what had happened.

The officer walked up to us. "My trooper here wants to shoot you, even without any evidence of your wrongdoing."
He seemed to be considering what to do. The soldier started

to speak, no doubt to press his case, but the officer held up his hand.

"We wouldn't want to harm such lovely ladies," he said, reaching over to touch my chin. I turned my head away. He moved closer and whispered in my ear. "You shouldn't be angry, mademoiselle," he hissed. "You have just experienced the might of German manhood."

He smiled and stepped back. "Kommandant," he said. The captain had decided to let the town commander determine our fate.

[Story picks up on page 12 of the original manuscript]

I leaned back in my chair, exhausted and angry at what had happened to Simone over fifty years ago. What a thing for a young woman to deal with. What a secret to keep all these years.

I spent a frustrating afternoon on the Internet. It was a long shot, but I thought I might be able to uncover the name of the man who had violated Simone.

The web site for the Library of Congress led me to the National Archives, the repository for a great many Nazi documents. It took an hour to discover that these files dealt with Germany itself, not the countries it had invaded.

I was looking for references to Le Croisic, Simone's home village, which the Germans occupied from 1940 until the end of the war. I hoped, perhaps foolishly, to find the names of the German officers assigned to that village.

Then, a telephone call to the French embassy in Washington yielded little more than rudeness until my call was transferred to a youngish-sounding woman in the office of the cultural attaché.

"I'm researching the effect of German occupation on small towns in your country," I said.

"Have you tried the Holocaust Memorial Center in Los Angeles?" she asked.

"No, I haven't."

I was vaguely aware of the Center, founded by a famous Nazi hunter.

"They have much archival material," the assistant said. "Perhaps someone there can help you, *monsieur*."

"That's a great idea, Miss . . ."

"Angelique Fontan."

"Miss Fontan. Thank you for the suggestion. I appreciate it."

"My pleasure to be of service, *monsieur*. I hope you find what you want. That was not a great period in the history of our country. Such a past needs to be illuminated as much as possible."

"I agree. Thank you very much."

Hanging up, I quickly located the web site of the center and trolled the directory until I found a heading named Occupied France. I located Le Croisic fairly quickly, with a growing sense of anticipation and excitement.

After general data about Brittany and the town appeared, a directory of other categories surfaced: Government Officials, History, Commerce, Resistance, and German Occupation. That listing contained a number of subcategories and one that seemed especially promising: German Garrison.

My attempt to open that file didn't get very far, however. As soon as I tried to open it, I got the message "Access Restricted." So much for swift and open research on the Internet. I returned to the home page and found a main telephone number. After dialing it, I was routed to a research librarian, who identified herself as Miss Stein.

"This is Tom Martindale. I'm a writer in Oregon doing research for a book on the effect of the German occupation on small towns in France during World War II," I said in my, by now, robotic spiel.

"Yes, Mr. Martindale," she said.

I waited for offers of help, but she said nothing. As was my usual habit with unexpected silence, I started to fill the void with words of my own—probably too many.

"I've heard that your center might have records of the German occupation of a particular town. I tried to find that material on your web site, but I encountered a snag." I waited. The silence on her end echoed in my ears. I even heard my stomach growl. "Miss Stein?"

"Yes, Mr. Martindale. What snag did you encounter?"

"Oh, yes, well . . . it was when I clicked onto the list of the German garrison in one town that I got an Access Restricted notation."

"And?"

"I called to see if I could get into the file. It would help me. I need those names for my book."

"That may be, Mr. Martindale, but we have our rules."

"But I thought your files were open to the public. If you don't let . . ."

"Please, may I finish?"

"Yes, of course. Sorry."

"If the file you want lists the names of German officers and enlisted men, access is restricted because there may be an ongoing investigation of one or more of the men on the list, and we don't wish to compromise that work."

"Oh, yes, I see. I had no idea."

"Few people do."

"Is there any way for me to get what I want?"

"You may request this list in writing, preferably on your official letterhead. You're with a magazine or newspaper?"

"Actually a university."

"Good, good. Our board tends to view academic institutions in a favorable light."

"Oh, so a board of some kind will review my letter then?"

"I was getting to that."

"Sorry. I don't mean to rush you."

"At any rate, our committee on archive access will review your letter and make its decision. Then, you'll get your list by return mail."

"How long will it take?"

"The committee meets twice a week. The next meeting is Monday. Address the letter to me—Rose Stein—at the main address."

"May I send it by fax?"

"Yes, but you will need to follow up with an original letter for our files, preferably certified, and be very precise as to what information you want, regarding which towns. If you can give me a FedEx account number, I will return the material to you as soon as possible."

"I appreciate your help," I said, giving her the number. "I'll get right on this and hope to hear from you soon. Thank you."

I hung up and immediately started composing my letter. I asked only for officer names of the garrison in Le Croisic from 1940 to 1945. I described my purpose—the bogus one of writing a book, not the real one of finding a murderer—and signed off. I attached my résumé to give the recipients an idea of who I was. I placed the material in a FedEx envelope, and I drove into town to drop it in a pickup box. On the way, I stopped at a stationery store and faxed a copy to Miss Stein.

The phone was ringing when I got back to my house an hour later. "Tom. It's Nate Golden. You sound out of breath."

"I was just coming in the door. I was going to call you."

"Something happen?"

"You might say that. Chuck Gates tried to kill me."

"That loony guy you knew before?"

"That's him."

I filled him in on what had happened at the aquarium.

"God, Tom. How'd he get near that shark tank?"

"His uncle said he'd done stories down at the aquarium and found out how to get in."

"You're lucky to be alive."

"Yeah, I guess so. I hope you can lock him up."

"I assume you will file a formal complaint."

"You bet. I see no other choice. Anyway, you called me . . ."

"Oh, yeah. We still can't find the Edwards kid."

I was tempted to reveal my suspicions about the rock quarry, but stopped short of that. I trusted Golden, but I felt a certain protective feeling toward Adam. I wasn't ready to throw him to the wolves yet.

"Is there anything you're not telling me, Tom?"

"No, Nate. You know I've hung up my detective's hat."

"From what Angela Pride tells me, that's not likely."

"When were you talking to her?"

"She's here right now. Want to talk to her?"

"Sure, I'd love to. But first, have you turned up anything on our German friends?"

"Not much. Neither has a record. Bader's personnel files at the university are confidential. Von Brandenberg's only been in the country a week. He's apparently here on vacation. I'm still checking. There's got to be more to them than this. I did find out that they rented a house for the summer up in Gleneden Beach—in Salishan, I think."

"That's interesting. It puts them over here all the time—not just occasional visits from Corvallis."

I quickly debated telling him about my call to the Holocaust Center. Why not? I had to trust somebody. I filled him in on my search and my conversation with Miss Stein.

"She sounds like my aunt," he laughed. "I hope you find what you are looking for. That center is supposed to be good at what they do—I mean, tracking down Nazis. Do you want to talk to Angela?"

I was surprised that he dropped the subject so abruptly.

"Sure, put her on the line. See you soon, Nate."

I could hear a muffled conversation before he handed her the phone.

"Hello, Tom."

"Is this the sexiest lieutenant in the Oregon State Police?"

"That's something only you would know, Professor Martindale, but I'm not at liberty to discuss it any further at this time."

It was wonderful to have broken through Angela's wall of humorlessness. I suspected I was one of the few people who had ever seen her drop that disciplined, orderly manner.

"That's something I'd love to explore at the earliest possible time."

"How about tonight. Dinner?"

I looked at my watch: 7:15 P.M.

"Tonight's not good for dinner. There's something I've got to do," I answered, thinking ahead to my trek to the quarry.

"Some sleuthing, no doubt," she laughed.

"Could we meet at my house later, maybe after midnight?"

"Sounds intriguing. Will little Jake be there?"

This really was a more relaxed Angela. I was amazed she'd use her name for my most private of parts in front of Golden.

"Is Nate still there?"

"No, he had to leave. You didn't answer my question, Tom."

I n the years after the Yaquina Head Outstanding Natural Area opened, operations in the rock quarry—which shared its headland—had ended. The reasons were complex and unclear. Some residents said it was because a powerful politician did not want to look at the quarry's scarred landscape from his summer home just down the coastline. Others said it resulted from worries over accidents when passenger cars driving to the lighthouse had to share the narrow road with gravel trucks and heavy equipment. Whatever the cause, most of the quarry's operations had been moved south of town several years ago. The property visible from the road still looked sadly barren, but not quite as scarred as before.

I waited until 9:30 P.M. to approach the entrance. Parking my car on an obscure side road, I walked the last half-mile over the headland. It was completely dark on the downside of the hill, and I stumbled now and then, using my flashlight only sporadically lest I attract the attention of a passing security guard or sheriff's patrol. As I got near the top of the ridge, I could see the skittering beams of light from the lighthouse beacon a mile to the northwest. That would make it easier when I got over the top.

Once there, I paused to look around, while hiding behind a pine tree for camouflage. I could make out several large pieces of equipment parked on a flat surface several hundred yards to my left. There were sheds that were open on one side and a larger building lay to my right up the hill and away from the other structures. This seemed the likely hideout for Adam Edwards. I hoped to find him sleeping like a baby inside.

I crept along the ridge and had almost reached the building when I noticed a dim light in the only window on the side facing me. I had to stand on my toes to look in. A kerosene lantern perched precariously on a small wooden box, and there was Adam Edwards, sitting on a stool reading a book he held close to his face. I eased around to the front of the building and knocked lightly on the door.

"Adam. Your mother sent me. I'm a friend." I tried the door, which opened easily.

"You know my momma?" He looked up, a calm expression on his face.

I stepped slowly inside. "Your momma sent me to help you. Let me take you home."

He stood and came toward me, a smile on his face. But at that moment, a beam of light streamed through the open door. I spun around to see a large earthmover bearing down on us fast. Its headlights glowed like the eyes of a demon as it rushed forward, its massive iron structure casting aside large boulders and chewing up whole sections of the ground in its path. The acrid smell of diesel filled the air.

I rolled on the ground to get out of the way just as the mechanical behemoth rushed by, flattening the building. I clawed my way up the gravel-covered hill, cutting my hands and tearing my clothes in the process.

I turned around to look back, my chest heaving as I struggled to catch my breath. The earthmover was already over the crest of the hill and down onto the road. I could hear the noise of its engine growing faint in the distance.

I calmed myself by closing my eyes and counting to ten, then I slowly eased down the hill. The dust was just beginning to settle as I switched on my flashlight and slowly inspected the shattered remains of the small wooden building. Adam was not there. Against all odds, he had escaped.

I picked through the boards with my foot and spotted something yellow. I reached down and picked up the book Adam had been reading. I dusted off the cover with my sleeve and read the title: *Learning to Read for Beginners.*

"Poor guy," I muttered to myself. "He's really trying."

I tucked the small volume under my arm and turned to walk away. As I did, the beam from my flashlight struck a bright object on the ground. I picked it up and ran my fingers over it.

A small metal button with the word "Benetton" gleamed in my hand.

Friday

What's that in your hand, Tom?" Angela asked, as she turned over and smiled at me sleepily.

"A button," I replied, handing it to her. I sat up on the edge of the bed, grabbed my robe, and stood up, turning around to face her. She was turning the button over in her fingers.

"Are you telling me you want me to sew this on something?" she laughed. "That could be very painful."

"Very painful," I said, quickly closing my robe. "It's actually a clue—or at least I think so. I'll tell you all about it over breakfast."

I headed for the bathroom and took a quick shower, making sure to keep my bandaged hand from getting wet. I dressed in jeans and a "Save the Whales" T-shirt and returned to the bedroom. Angela was sitting up, a sheet pulled across her breasts.

"I really like the new, unbuttoned Angela," I said. "I've never seen you this relaxed before. I mean, when we were together before, things never went this well. I'm glad you came over last night. It made me realize how much I've missed you." I walked over to the bed and kissed her.

"Things were just about perfect," she said, a dreamy look in her eyes.

The night before had gone better than I expected. Maybe it was because I felt so comfortable with Angela now.

"I've got to get moving," she said, suddenly becoming the brisk, efficient state police lieutenant as she picked up her watch from the night stand. "I'm supposed to be at a training seminar in Astoria by noon." She waved me away. "I'll get showered and dressed, and you can tell me about this clue." She handed the button back to me and got up, the sheet draped around her stunning body.

I was just putting eggs and bacon on two plates when she walked into the kitchen fifteen minutes later. I pointed to a chair as I filled her coffee cup and placed a stack of buttered toast on the table between us. She tucked a napkin into her shirt collar and started to eat.

"I need to be spotless for the troops," she laughed, pointing at her immaculate uniform. "Is your hand better today? I can't believe that lunatic put you through all of that. You say Nate is picking him up?"

"Yes to both questions. I don't think I'll have to worry about Gates anymore. He's so nuts he'll be locked up for a long time."

"Good. Now, what about that button?"

I pulled it out of my pocket and held it up between two fingers. "It says 'Benetton' on it, did you notice?"

"Means nothing to me," she replied, between bites.

"It's an Italian clothing company known for running provocative ads in magazines. They believe in publicizing causes like world hunger and AIDS—even men on death row—as much as selling their latest creations. It got people to thinking about things they'd just as soon ignore. I really admire that campaign."

"How does that button become a clue?"

"I found it last night after an . . . incident. The . . . a . . . person involved in the incident must have lost it off his shirt or jacket. It just strikes me as odd that anyone in Newport, Oregon, would own clothes from that manufacturer. I doubt if any stores even sell it here. That should make it easy to locate."

Angela finished eating and was dabbing her mouth with the napkin she had removed from her collar. "And why would you want to locate that person? And what is this incident you keep referring to?"

"Somebody tried to run me over with an earthmover last night at the rock quarry."

Angela's eyes widened, and her eyebrows arched. "I doubt I'm going to be happy when I hear this story, but go on."

"You've got to promise I'm talking to Angela Pride, friend and sometime lover of Tom Martindale, not Angela Pride, Oregon State Police lieutenant."

"For now," she said. "But I can't guarantee I'll stay that way."

I threw caution to the winds and told Angela everything—from the moment Simone invited me to brunch to what happened at the rock quarry. She listened intently and didn't interrupt.

"Did you tell Nate Golden about any of this?" she asked when I finished.

"Some of it. A couple of times he was involved after the fact—I mean the ransacking of Simone's study and Connie Wright's murder."

"What about the Edwards guy? What's his name, Adam?"

"Yeah, Adam. No, I didn't say anything about my suspicions. I've felt very protective of Adam since I first heard about him. I've been trying to find the real killer so Adam won't be a part of this. If you met him you'd know instantly that he couldn't kill anyone. He's just not capable of anything like that. What's more, he wouldn't be able to figure out how to cover it up."

I took a sip of coffee, trying to determine Angela's reactions to my withholding of evidence. She was, after all, a cop.

"Why do you get yourself into messes like this?" she said, exasperated. "Do you think you have to prove something to the world?"

She was probably right, but I wasn't ready to admit it. Maybe I did take foolish chances to compensate for other failings.

"I'm sorry, Tom. I shouldn't have said that," she whispered, patting my hand. "You always want to help the underdog, and that's admirable. You just need to think twice before you go off half . . ." She blushed and looked away.

"Half-cocked?" I laughed. "How can you say that after last night? Are you going to help me or tell Nate?"

She didn't say anything for a long time; she just sat there drinking coffee and looking out the window toward the sea. "I'll give you three days to sort this out, Tom. I'll go to my training session and then come back through Newport. If you haven't turned up anything by then, we'll go to Nate together, acting like you just told me what you'd been doing. It's risky, but I'll do it because I know you well enough to trust your judgment. I'd call a halt to this sooner if I had time. You've got to promise that you'll do what I say, Tom. Don't tell me what I want to hear, then do something stupid. My job could be at risk here."

"I appreciate what you're doing. I promise." I got up and walked around, leaning down to kiss her. She returned my kiss passionately, then pulled away. "I've got to be on the road," she said, standing up and running her hands down her uniform to smooth out any wrinkles. She grabbed her overnight bag and walked to the door.

"I enjoyed last night a lot, Tom. I feel safe with you. I need to feel that way sometimes."

I followed her outside, surprised by her candor. "I'm glad you came, Angela. I've really missed you. Thanks." She blew me a kiss and got into her car. I waved as she drove away.

After I cleaned up the kitchen, I called Rose Edwards.

"Glad to hear from you, Mr. Martindale. I was beginning to worry. Have you found my Adam?"

"As a matter of fact, I did, Rose. For a moment."

"Where is he?"

"I found him at that shack in the rock quarry. We started to talk, but someone came, and he ran away." It seemed best not to burden her with all the gory details.

"Ran where?" asked Rose, starting to cry.

"I hoped you could tell me. He can't go to the cemetery. Where else would he go?"

"Oh, Lord, my poor boy." Rose was sobbing now.

"Rose, listen to me. Adam is a survivor. He may be slow, but he seems to have developed a keen instinct to survive. I'll bet he's probably always faced bullies."

"Yes," she said quietly, blowing her nose. "How did you know?"

"Just a guess. The same skills that helped him with those idiotic bullies is helping him outwit the rest of us now." I believed what I said. I wasn't ready to write Adam Edwards off, and neither should his mother.

"I hope you're right."

"Look, Rose, I've got to go. Call me on my cell phone if Adam turns up. You have the number?"

"Yes, I wrote it down last week when you called madame. Here it is."

"All right. Keep in touch. And one other thing. Have the Germans been around?"

"No, but Mr. Bader called and left his number in case I needed to reach him."

She gave me the number and we hung up. As I sat there contemplating my next move, I thought of a way I might find out
all I needed to know about Bader and von Brandenberg without waiting for whatever was in the Holocaust Center archive.

For most residents on the Oregon coast, the Salishan Spit
seemed like a proverbial accident waiting to happen. The
thin strip of sand extending into the Pacific was vulnerable to
storms. But like the barrier islands off the southeastern U.S.,
that vulnerability had not prevented developers from building
large, expensive homes on the Spit. Luck and the placement of
large boulders offshore had prevented catastrophe—so far. But
each winter storm brought renewed fears that this time the Spit
would be breached and some of the houses would go floating
out to sea like huge Spanish galleons.

After a quick call to a friend at the phone company, I was
able to find the address of the house on the Spit that Bader was
renting. Before I left home, I called Nate Golden. I decided to
follow Angela's advice and fill him in with what I knew—at
least to a point. When he didn't answer, I left a brief message.

I parked my car in the large parking lot of Salishan's
Marketplace Mall and headed onto the golf course. The area
was restricted to golfers or guests at the Lodge across Highway
101, but I could easily be either in my sporty outfit. No one
challenged me as I made my way along the path to the beach.
Once there, I could walk north to the area adjacent to the
homes because all Oregon beaches are public. I joined a smat-
tering of beachcombers. Each new tide brought small rocks
and shells onto the fine black sand. I walked near the water's
edge to make better time, since the drier sand was so deep that
even a short stroll turned into an exhausting trudge.

It took me fifteen minutes to walk the half-mile to where I thought the house was located. It was supposed to be on Ocean Wind Lane at the very end. I hadn't yet figured out what I would do once I got there. I'd just wait to see what happened. In my experience, opportunities always present themselves.

I headed toward the houses on that street, pausing in the sand dunes to look out to sea and to the north and south, so I'd appear to be a tourist. Luckily for me, few people had ventured this far. I could see a man and a woman with a large dog far to the north. Nearby, a woman and two small children were building a sand castle. Except for them, I was alone.

I brought my binoculars to my face and made the same reconnoiter: sea, south, and north. I walked farther into the dunes and sat down, pulling out a paperback book I planned to pretend to be reading. *Seabirds of the Pacific Northwest* would not have been my normal choice, but it served as ideal camouflage now.

I remained still for several minutes, then dared to look at the houses to my east. They were all built in what realtors called New England saltbox style: wooden, shingled, gray with plain fronts and slanting roofs. I scanned the area looking for anyone familiar. At first, my search yielded nothing. I saw no people or movement of any kind. A second look was more successful. There was a BMW pulling into a driveway and Bader's wife, Elaine, was getting out. She entered one of the houses at the end of the street, adjacent to the sand.

There was no way to tell if she was alone or how long she would stay—I would have to wait. The time dragged by, as I pretended to consult my bird book and look out to sea now and then. The wind, normally brisk on most days, was thankfully quiet today. I thought I would hear the car start if anyone left.

Eleven. Noon. My stomach was beginning to churn. I felt like a cop on stakeout, but a very nervous one. I wasn't used to spending my time doing this kind of thing. Maybe I did need to leave investigating to the real detectives and get back to what I knew best: teaching and writing.

Just as I was beginning to consider leaving, I heard a door slam. Through my binoculars I spotted Bader, his wife, and von Brandenberg head toward the car. The men were carrying suitcases and Elaine Bader was locking the front door. She tried the doorknob several times, to be sure it was securely locked.

What luck. They were obviously leaving for a long enough time that I could search the house without fear of discovery. After a flurry of slamming trunk lids and doors, they got inside, and the car drove away. I waited another ten minutes before venturing up and over the sand dune.

I kept up my pretense, pausing to look at the ocean and examining a flock of circling seagulls meandering above me. As with many homes on the Spit, the other three on the street were used by their wealthy owners for only a few weeks each year. And right now, even though it was summer, they looked deserted.

I crossed to the main road and turned back, pretending to return to the dunes and beach. But just as I passed the Bader house, I darted behind a tall hedge and hurried around to the rear of the building. The dunes and sea grass would give me the cover I needed.

The shades were drawn on all of the large windows and two sliding doors. I was about to reconsider my plan when I noticed that a small window of frosted glass had been left open. Summoning the experience I had gained at the cemetery the week before, I used a patio table to climb up to the window and slip through.

I held onto the handhold for the shower and swung my legs down onto the tile floor of a large bathroom, then I eased to the door and out into a hall. Every few moments I stopped to listen for any sounds in the house, even though I was certain everyone had driven away.

The hall opened onto two other rooms, then led to the front door. The living room and adjacent dining room were next to the main entrance. Both were full of boxes, some empty, some in need of unpacking; the Baders were still in the process of moving in. I walked back to two closed doors I had passed. The first was a bedroom whose occupant hadn't finished unpacking.

The next room was the study I hoped to find. It was small, with shelves containing bric-a-brac and a few books. Even in the chaos of moving in, Bader had set up his office. A desk held a computer, and a printer stood on a side table. I sat down in front of the computer and booted it up. Bader had made it easy for me. Not expecting an intruder to come in during his absence, he had left his disks out. I didn't have to shuffle through the stack very long before finding something promising: a disk marked "Family Memoirs." I inserted it and scrolled through the directory, stopping to open the file holding the introduction.

Bader and his cousin were working on a history of their family, from its beginning in Germany in the 1880s to the present. A family tree showed their connections to royalty before World War I. The narrative detailed great wealth accumulated over the years from ownership of a number of factories that built everything from carriages to automobiles to airplane parts. I returned to the directory and brought up the file for World War II. The chapter contained only a few pages of vague language and details that could be obtained in any general reference work.

Returning to the directory, I discovered a file I had missed on my first pass: "Progress Report." This contained a chart detailing the status of the book's chapters. Of the twenty-five, only eight were marked complete with an X. In the grid for Chapter

18—on World War II entitled "A Fortune in Decline"—an X appeared in only two categories: "Interviews Requested" and "Family Records Received."

A special note at the bottom also related to this chapter; "S G *Memoiren*—To Be Added" probably referred to Simone's memoir. It was as if Bader expected to find additional details in her autobiography pertinent to the history of his family. There were so many questions I simply could not answer. For one thing, why would he think the memoir would be useful if he hadn't read it or Simone hadn't told him about it? Was the German officer who raped Simone a relative of Bader and von Brandenberg? If so, was fear of exposing his identity great enough for either—or both—of them to resort to murder to keep the details hidden? A Nazi lurking in his past certainly wouldn't do his career any good. Perhaps the two had learned the family's dirty secret in whatever family records they had obtained. They were probably so inconclusive they needed more details to verify their suspicions. After all, they hadn't yet written the chapter itself.

Finding those family records would probably give me all I needed. Where had they hidden them? And what was I looking for—old leather-bound diaries, microfilmed documents, packets of letters? I found nothing in the desk drawers. The room contained no filing cabinets. I couldn't tear the rest of the house apart when I didn't even know what I was looking for. I sat down in the chair and reached over to turn off the computer, my back to the door.

"Vot haf ve here, *Herr* Martindale?" said a voice behind me. "An intruder in our midst?"

"I don't know what to say." I muttered, as I slowly turned to face the shadowy figure in the doorway.

"How about promising not to do this again?" Nate Golden stepped into the room, smiling. He was in civilian clothes.

"Nate. God, you scared the shit out of me." I sank back into the chair, my knees shaking. "I thought it was our German pals."

"Look, Tom. Let's get out of here right now before someone finds us both."

I didn't argue, just followed Golden into the dining room and out the sliding door. The street was deserted as we walked over the sand dunes toward the beach. We didn't speak until we were safely on the sand heading south.

"Slow down, Nate. I can't hold a conversation with someone who's running a marathon."

He motioned toward a large piece of driftwood wedged into a sand hill to our left, and sat down. "I don't suppose you realize the seriousness of what you did, Tom. You may think you're . . ."

"I know, I know. You already said that. I just get . . ."

"Let me finish, please. You always think you're on the side of truth and justice, but the rest of the world may not see it that way. You almost got your ass in the biggest sling it's ever been in. From what Angela Pride tells me, that's your modus operandi.

"You talked to Angela about me, again?"

"In passing, yeah. I've been trying to figure out how to deal with you while I conduct my murder investigations. You know, Tom, this kind of stunt doesn't make my job any easier."

"I know, I know." I hung my head in contrition. I saw his point.

"What possessed you to break into that house?" he asked.

"Bader's renting it, and when I discovered that, I decided to see if I could find out anything."

"Find out what? If he kept a murder confession on his hard drive?" Golden said.

"I've got this theory that these two Germans are somehow linked to someone or something in Simone Godard's past. I did find something on his computer—part of a family history. He even made a notation to consult her memoir. That's why he broke into her house and maybe killed her and Connie Wright. It's all in the memoir."

"Whoa. Hang on, Tom. You're moving too fast for me. You may have suspicions, but that's not the kind of proof I'd need to make an arrest and get it to pass muster with the D.A."

"Well, it's a start. Wouldn't you at least admit that?"

He nodded reluctantly.

"Okay. Good. We can move on . . ."

"Wait a minute, Tom. I don't like this 'we' stuff. How many times do I have to tell you, this is a police matter? It doesn't involve you in any way. I should probably arrest you for 'B and

E,' just to get you out of my hair." He was smiling, so I knew he wasn't serious. But he was angry at me, no doubt about it.

"How did you know I was here? Did you get my message?"

"No, it's my day off so I hadn't checked my voice mail. I was in the Salishan Marketplace having coffee. I saw you park, and I was almost going to call you over to join me. But then I saw you head onto the golf course, so I decided to follow you instead."

"You watched me all that time I waited in the dunes?" I shook my head in disbelief.

"You learn patience in my business. It comes from lots of hours on stakeouts."

"So, you could have stopped my 'B and E'? Why didn't you?" I was smiling, but it was a serious question.

"Don't try to turn me into an accomplice, Tom. Who do you think people would believe, you or an Oregon State Police sergeant?"

The conversation was taking an odd turn I didn't think I liked. "I was just asking, Nate. It was just a thought."

He relaxed and smiled, his old benevolent self returning. "You just make me crazy with all your nosing around."

By the time we parted an hour later, I had filled him in on everything I knew about the Germans. He fixed on every word, commenting on my findings as I spoke by saying things like "Okay, yes," "That makes sense," "I didn't know that," and "Yes, I knew that."

I didn't say anything about my encounter with the earth-mover. That would only bring on another lecture—the last thing I wanted to hear now.

efore I returned to my car, I bought a copy of *The Depoe Bay Whaler*. I unlocked the door and slid in behind the wheel, scanning the front page for something I hoped I'd see. I wasn't disappointed.

WHALER *erred in reporting murder*

In a story in last week's edition, Thomas Martindale of Newport was listed as a suspect in the apparent murder of Simone Godard, a resident of Depoe Bay.

According to a spokesperson for County Sheriff Art Kutler, Martindale has no involvement in this death. The Depoe Bay Whaler regrets this error and any implications drawn from it about Martindale or anyone else.

I would save this retraction and show it to anyone who asked. Making a bigger fuss would only attract attention. Letting it die quietly was the best thing for me. In public relations, they call that a "one-day story." If a person was lucky, a story appeared, made its splash, then went away. I was feeling happy with the way this had worked out, as I started my car and headed south down Highway 101.

It was just before 3 P.M. when I pulled up in front of the newspaper office. The same woman was on duty behind the counter, and she knew why I was there before I said a word.

"Mr. Gates," she said into her antiquated intercom, "That Mr. Martingale is here." A definite bond had been created between us, I was certain of that.

"Thanks for remembering me," I said sweetly.

"I always remember the troublemakers," she said unsmilingly, as she led me through the swinging door.

The ancient Mr. Gates was sitting behind his equally ancient desk as I entered. He looked sick.

"Don't get up," I said, gesturing for him to sit still. "Are you feeling all right?"

"I don't feel so good, my boy. My tests didn't come out so good. I was going to call you—I don't mean about the tests. I wondered if . . ."

"I'm happy with the retraction? Yes, very happy. Thank you for running it. I think my reputation will survive intact now." I was smiling, but Gates's face still looked grim.

"That's not what I was going to say. Of course you liked the retraction. It's word-for-word the way you dictated it to me."

"Sorry. I interrupted you. What were you going to say?"

"My nephew Chuck is missing. He's a scoundrel, but my sister expects me to look after him. I've let her down. The police were here looking for him, too." He seemed on the verge of tears. He wiped a hand across his face as if to erase the unpleasantness he expected when it came to talking about his nephew. Charles Gates had more than one screw loose in his head, but I didn't wish him any harm. And I really liked this old man.

"Tell me what you know, and maybe I can help you."

Gates's face relaxed. "I haven't seen him since that day you came in here. You remember I yelled for him. The girls said he ran out the back. He called me late that night and said he was in some trouble and had to lie low for a few days. He asked for an advance on his salary in cash."

"How did you get it to him?"

"He had me leave it in an envelope under a flower pot on my porch. I tried to stay awake so I could talk to him, but taking this medicine and all, I really conk out at night. When I woke up in the morning, the envelope was gone."

I didn't want to make this kind old man feel any worse than he already did by mentioning that I had seen his nephew's car at Connie Wright's or what he had tried to do to me at the aquarium. Other people would be dealing with that.

"Mr. Gates, this could be exactly what it looks like. Chuck needed to get away for a few days, nothing more."

"Part of me wants to believe that. Will you help me?"

"I'm not a detective, Mr. Gates."

"But you teach investigative reporting, don't you? That's like detective work." The old man was pleading. "It would make a real good story. Maybe you could write it up and sell it to one of the tabloids. I'd really appreciate your help. I'm just not up to doing this on my own."

The private detective and his seventy-five-year-old assistant. Wouldn't Nate Golden and Angela Pride get a laugh out of that?

"Sure, I'll help. Why don't we start by checking Chuck's house to see if we find anything."

"Now you're talking." He suddenly seemed energized, the illness and depression cast aside. "Wanda," he barked into the intercom, "I'm going out for a while."

Gates got up and grabbed a cap that was hanging on a nearby rack. He jammed it onto his head with one hand and stuffed an unlit cigar into his mouth with the other. "We can go out my private entrance back here."

I followed him down a short hall and through a door that took us to a small parking lot containing only one vehicle: a gold Cadillac Coupe de Ville with the longest fins I'd ever seen. He unlocked the driver's door and got in, while I slid in on the passenger side. Gates brought the engine to life, and it is not an exaggeration to say it was purring. Soon air-conditioning had cooled the immaculate interior, and he was backing out into the alley.

"This is quite a car," I said. "Bet you bought it new."

"Yes, sir, I did. In 1958. It's been a keen car. The only thing I've had to do is install a newer engine a few years ago to make it more fuel efficient."

By now, we were out of the alley and turning east up a steep hill away from the highway.

"I've never been up here. It's quite beautiful—I mean, with that view of the ocean and all."

"It'll be that way until all those damned developers get their hands on it. They'll rape those hills just like the timber companies did. Then we'll have mud slides down below and a bunch of cheap-looking A-frames up here."

We drove up and over the hillside and headed down into a small valley. The trees were so dense they blocked out traffic noise even this close to the highway. I rolled down the window to let the clean, pungent smell of pine waft in.

"I moved a small mobile home onto a lot I own back here and let Chuck live in it rent free. We'll turn onto the access road up there by that post. It's back in the trees a few hundred yards."

"Pardon me for asking, Mr. Gates, but why didn't you drive back here and check on Chuck before?"

"I guess I don't have the courage I used to have. I've been stewing around about what to do for a day or so. When you showed up this afternoon, I realized you were someone I could ask to help. I sized you up the other day as a smart young fellow who knows his way around."

"I'm flattered that you put so much faith in me, but don't get your hopes up. We really need to call in the police if Chuck turns out to be missing."

"I guess you're right. I've known that jackass sheriff, Art Kutler, for twenty years. He couldn't find a diamond in a patch of black gravel, but maybe some of the other cops aren't as dumb."

I smiled at Gates's assessment.

We soon reached the trailer. He made no move to get out, but handed me a key. "Would you mind, Mr. Martingale? Look. His car is parked over there."

"Sure, but come as far as the door. You know your nephew doesn't like me very much. It will be better if he can see you with me."

He nodded and got out. We walked the few hundred yards to the entrance together. I eased up the wooden steps and inserted the key into the lock. The stench that drifted out of the door when I opened it made me gasp for breath.

"Stay here, Mr. Gates."

I stepped into a kitchen area. The sink was piled high with dishes, roaches crawling over tiny remnants of food. I flipped a light switch with no success. Gates probably hadn't paid his bill. As my eyes tried to get used to the dark, I stumbled over a lot of bottles lined up along the short hall to the rear. I picked one up and looked at the label: Mexican beer.

I stepped into the living room and tried another switch. Oddly, the lights worked in this room. My brain couldn't quite comprehend what my eyes were seeing: photos of me tacked onto a long cork bulletin board. Some had been taken at my house, one as I walked along the road, another at the lighthouse, another at the Fred Meyer store, still another outside Simone's house as I was talking to Nate Golden. Chuck Gates had been stalking me for weeks, and the thought sickened me. I forced myself not to touch any of the papers on a nearby card table.

The smell got stronger as I neared a closed door at the end of the room. I placed a handkerchief over my nose as I pushed open the puny door with one foot.

I saw the blood splattered on the wall above the bed before I saw Gates.

26

felt no satisfaction about the mutilated body slumped in front of me—only horror. I broke into a sweat and felt weak in my knees. Then I remembered the old man outside and his bad heart.

When I stepped out the door, Merle Gates was leaning against the hood of his gold Caddie. He sensed the bad news before I said anything.

"Is he in there?" He started toward the mobile home, but I caught him gently by the shoulders.

"Just stay out here, Mr. Gates. We've got to call the police."

"So Chuck's dead. Oh, God, what am I going to tell my sister?" He started to cry. "She's always watched over me. Now I've let her down."

I eased him to the car and opened the passenger side door so he could sit down. His eyes were filled with tears, his lower lip quivering.

"I need to get to a phone."

"There's one of those cell things under the seat there, I think. I never go in much for new-fangled gadgets, but my doctor talked me into getting it in case I got sick on the road." He reached down and pulled out a gleaming new cell phone and handed it to me. "Can you work it?"

I quickly dialed Nate Golden's number. He wasn't back on duty, and he wasn't picking up at home. I dreaded calling 911 because I knew the Sheriff's Department would respond.

Two sheriff patrol cars answered my call within ten minutes. I could see their lights flashing through the trees long before their vehicles became visible. The deputy who had pulled me over the week before was driving the first unit; a woman I had never seen was in the second. The two officers ran toward me with hands on their holsters.

"Don't I know you?" the male deputy said.

"I don't think so," I lied.

"You called this in, Mr. . . ." the female deputy consulted a slip of paper. "Mr. Martindale?"

"Yes, I did. This is Merle Gates, editor of the local newspaper. We came to visit his nephew, Charles Gates. I found him inside." I glanced over at Merle Gates's face. "Can we move over there and talk? Mr. Gates is feeling pretty bad."

She nodded, and the three of us headed over to the mobile home.

"I found his nephew's body inside. It looks to me like he blew his head off with a shotgun."

The male officer suddenly became energized as the sound of my voice must have triggered something in his memory.

"You're the guy I pulled over last week. The one Sheriff Kutler warned me about." He turned to the woman. "Maybe we should have him assume the position and pat him down."

She looked at him in complete disbelief. "Pat him down for what, Larry? Concealing a dangerous cell phone? He's the citizen who called in this incident."

She shook her head and gave me a look that seemed to say I should overlook this idiot's lack of good judgment. "Let's see what we've got. Please wait here, Mr. Martindale."

They both drew their revolvers and stepped inside. She soon returned.

"We'll need statements from you and Mr. Gates. Is he all right?"

"He's got a heart condition. Could I take him home?"

"I don't see why not. You're local, right?"

"Yeah, I live in Newport."

"We'll get his statement tomorrow. Will you come in to our headquarters then, too, and let us ask you a few questions? It sure looks like suicide to me."

I was grateful for this woman's good sense, but surprised she hadn't made the connection between me and all the photos on Chuck Gates's board. Needless to say, I was only too happy to maneuver the big Caddie out of the driveway and down the hill.

"Poor Bernice, my poor sister," Merle Gates kept muttering, as we drove along.

I parked his car behind the newspaper building and helped him inside to his office. Once seated behind his desk, he seemed to throw off his despondent mood. "Wanda, will you come into my office, please," Gates barked into his intercom. "We've got a story to cover," I heard him say, as I left the building.

Later, back home, I sat at my desk trying to sort out the significance of Gates's death. Had he killed himself in an act of remorse over killing Simone and Connie Wright? And why had he killed them? Was it linked to his hatred of me? If he was trying to frame me for those murders, he hadn't established a link anyone would believe. Was that why he had lured me to the aquarium and tried to kill me?

None of it made any sense, but I guess Chuck Gates hadn't acted rationally for years.

It was hard to throw off another persistent thought: some evidence pointed to the Germans as Simone's killers. I might be influenced by a lifetime of watching World War II movies with Nazis as the villains, but Bader and von Brandenberg seemed much more likely suspects than Gates.

The trill of my cell phone broke my concentration. It was Nate Golden.

"So you're in trouble again, Tom."

"How'd you find out?"

"It's on the police radio."

"So, is the sheriff about to swoop in on me?" I laughed.

"It's nothing to snicker over, Tom. They found that shrine to you in Gates's trailer. I'm sure Kutler has some questions. I'm surprised that deputy let you go."

"Wait a minute. All of that was on the radio? Nate, were you trailing Gates or were you watch . . ."

"I'll explain when I see you. Do you know the mortuary and cemetery south of town near the exit from the bridge? I've found out some interesting things about the owner and his partner. I also got a line on Adam Edwards. He's got a little cottage on the grounds. I'm there now."

"Is Adam safe?"

"I can't say any more on the phone, Tom. I'll fill you in when you get here."

"I'll leave right away."

I hung up and grabbed my keys, now more certain than ever that Nate had been following me. On the way out, I noticed

the distinctive purple and orange markings of a FedEx overnight package on the porch behind a planter. I was glad I had
filed a signature card card so I didn't have to be here to sign for
the delivery. In my haste to get inside, I hadn't seen it. I tucked
it under my arm after noting the return address: the Holocaust
Memorial Center in Los Angeles. I'd read it later.

27

The Yaquina Bay Bridge is an architectural gem, a 3,223-foot long series of steel arches that connects one part of Newport to the other. Built in 1936 by the same engineer who designed all the many spans along Highway 101 on the Oregon coast, this bridge has nifty-looking Art Deco pylons to set off its high center arch. Before the bridges were built, drivers along what was then called the Pacific Coast Highway had to cross the broad, flat estuaries that dot the long coastline by ferry or make a run for it at low tide.

I was reading all this information on a sign on the northern approach to the bridge where I'd been stuck in traffic for ten minutes. The salt air damages all the coastal bridges, so repair work is ongoing and often done at night when traffic is light. Highway workers move banks of bright lights into place and go about their tasks high above the roadway. Unfortunately, all traffic must be stopped from time to time in the process. Noticing that drivers ahead of me had shut off their engines and gotten out of their cars, I had given in as well. The delay would at least give me time to look at the Holocaust Center material. Miss Stein may have been prickly to deal with, but she was thorough. She had included about fifty pages of documentation and highlighted them for me. She hadn't even waited for my official letter.

"Mr. Martindale," said a letter attached to page one, "I decided to expedite your request, and the process went faster than I thought it would. You may be particularly interested in pages seventeen, twenty-four, and forty-six. Good hunting."

Using the penlight I kept in my glove box for illumination, I turned to the first reference, an analysis of the German occupation of Le Croisic, France, from 1940 to 1945:

> *The German garrison at Le Croisic, France, a small fishing village about four hundred kilometers southwest of Paris, was no better or no worse than the actions of the Nazi regime all over non-Vichy France during the Second World War.*
>
> *The commandant for most of the time was Colonel Hans Stuber, an officer in the German army and not a party member. As a result, the atrocities committed against Jews, Gypsies, and others deemed "undesirable" by leaders in Berlin were not as widespread in this area as in the rest of France under German occupation.*
>
> *That is not to say that life was easy for French people living in Le Croisic or that everything was serene. An active cell of the French Resistance kept the Germans on their toes by committing acts of sabotage such as blowing up bridges and setting fire to warehouses. Members of the cell also published and distributed a newspaper and exchanged clandestine messages via a radio transmitter. The radio was hidden in the cellar of a lighthouse operated by August Godard, and never found by the Germans. His daughter, Simone, distributed the newspaper. (She later worked for the Resistance while a university student in Paris.)*

> *To root out such defiance, Stuber assigned various staff officers. The most ruthless was Captain Fritz von Brandenberg, a dedicated member of the Nazi Party, who was shot in 1945 when he tried to crash through an American roadblock.*

Bingo. The current Fritz von Brandenberg and his cousin, the university's own Fred Bader, were doing everything they could to keep their relative's wartime deeds quiet. One or the other of them must have killed Simone and Connie Wright to get the memoir. I couldn't wait to tell Nate Golden.

Traffic was still not moving. There would be time to read on.

> *A key member of the Resistance cell in the nearby city of St. Nazaire was a Jew, Marcel Goldenberg. Goldenberg, a law student, was particularly daring in his defiance of the Germans. He led a number of raids on trucks and warehouses. His group also blew up a key railroad bridge.*

> *His zeal resulted, in part, from revenge. His young wife and infant son were taken prisoner in 1943 during a search for him. When he didn't turn himself in as demanded by the Germans to secure their release, the young woman and baby were shot on direct orders of Captain von Brandenberg.*

That bastard. Simone had had a rough time, but at least lived to tell her story. Or had she? Knowledge of those old murders in wartime had probably gotten her killed these many years later. I turned to the last page Miss Stein had marked. It was headed "Whereabouts of Principals/St. Nazaire Region." In the von Brandenberg listing, I quickly found what I was looking for. Under family members still living, two names stood out: Fritz von Brandenberg, grandson, Munich, Germany; and Manfred Bader, great nephew, Corvallis, Oregon.

"Trying to keep an old skeleton buried," I muttered to myself. I read another key listing:

> *Marcel Goldenberg: emigrated to United States, 1947; U.S. citizen, 1949; married Lena Hier, 1952, two children, five grandchildren; worked as attorney in Brooklyn, New York until his death in 1980. Changed name to Golden in 1953.*

That last entry stopped me cold.

28

As if on cue, the traffic on my side of the highway started moving. While drivers raced to their vehicles and started their engines, I put my car in gear and headed south, hoping I was wrong about a friend I had trusted completely.

I made it across the bridge at a normal forty-five miles per hour. Like on my earlier visit to the cemetery, I drove down Highway 101, passing the entrance to both it and the mortuary. I planned to park my car in a rest area to the south and walk back. I wasn't sure what I'd find and decided it was best to arrive unannounced.

As I had the week before, I walked through the grove of shore pines to the edge of the cemetery, then continued up the slight incline to the building where Adam Edwards lived from time to time. I could see a dim light shining through the bathroom window I had slithered through before. This time, I'd go through the front door like a normal person. I was tired of skulking around. It was slightly ajar, and I could see Nate Golden looking at some papers in front of him.

"Nate," I said quietly, as I pushed the door open.

"Tom, it's you. Good. Come on in and sit down."

I sat down on the bed. "Where's Adam Edwards? I thought you'd found him."

"Not exactly, but I think this is where he's been hiding out."

"I know he must be scared shitless over all of this. I can't say I blame . . ." I started saying.

"I also found out why he killed your friend Madame Godard and Connie Wright."

"Adam. A killer? I don't believe . . ."

"I've got strong evidence right here." As he stepped toward me, I noticed what he was wearing: jeans, a black polo shirt, and a khaki jacket that looked expensive.

"Nate, I've rarely seen you out of uniform," I said casually. "That's quite a jacket. I like it."

"Thanks, Tom. I got it in Israel."

That revelation got my attention. As he leaned over and placed the papers he had been reading in my lap, I noticed one of the buttons on his jacket was missing, leaving only a frayed thread where it had been.

"Look at this stuff, Tom. It shows that Lyle Chapman, the mortician, and Verne Andrews, your friend's attorney, were trying to buy both the houses in Depoe Bay to expand their operations."

"What houses?"

"Both the Godard and Wright houses."

"Expand their operations how?"

Golden didn't answer.

"What did Adam have to do with a scheme like that?"

"He was their hit man. They hired him to kill both women, then made sure I found him out."

"I can't believe . . ."

"Adam didn't kill Madame Simone. Madame Simone was Adam's friend." The voice and the child-like phrases were familiar. Adam Edwards quickly stepped out of the bathroom. He was bigger and more muscular than I had realized.

"Hold it right there, Edwards," shouted Nate, pulling his gun. "I'm arresting you for the murder of Simone Godard and Connie Wright."

"Nate, stop all this shit right now," I said, forgetting who held the gun.

He instantly motioned Adam over to where I was, and now included me in his gun sight. I plunged ahead, doubting he would actually pull the trigger.

"Why'd you kill them, Nate? To get the manuscript? And why did you try to kill me at the quarry?"

"How did you figure that out?"

I reached into my pocket and held up the button. "I guess you lost it on that earthmover."

"You're pretty smart, Tom, but not making any sense," said Golden, still holding the gun on us. "Why would I care about some old war memoir? They're a dime a dozen."

"Because your grandfather's first wife and child were murdered by the Nazis in St. Nazaire. You were doing this for your grandfather. I think we both know that our German friends are related to the principal Nazi hit man in that town."

"Tom. This is ridiculous," he said, laughing uneasily, as if someone had told a joke he didn't believe was very funny. "My head's about to burst. I need time to think . . ." He rubbed his forehead. "I didn't mean to kill either of them. They were just too stubborn."

He stopped talking and his eyes hardened, the soft, pleading look of seconds before suddenly becoming all steely. "I want you both to face the wall while I put these cuffs on you."

"Nate, don't do . . ."

"Tom," he cut me off. "Move it."

We did as we were told, but as Adam Edwards turned, he suddenly lashed out at Golden, knocking him off balance. The gun went off, a bullet smashing the overhead light.

"Adam, run!" I yelled, as I rushed for the door. As I sprinted across the lawn, I could hear shouting behind me and another shot.

I didn't worry about desecrating graves or tripping over tombstones, just raced across the cemetery as fast as I could. Getting back to my car was out of the question from this direction, so I decided to take my chances to the north, where I might flag down a passing car.

The lights were out in the mortuary as I ran past. I headed down the driveway and onto Highway 101, stopping to catch my breath at the side of the road. I used my sleeve to wipe the dripping sweat off my face. I couldn't see a car in either direction, so I started toward a bank of lights where a group of men were working in the middle of the bridge.

I picked up my pace and started waving my arms. I was still too far away for them to hear me. Suddenly a bullet zinged past my right ear, and I veered to the side, hiding behind the base of one of the stone pillars. I slowly poked my head around just in time to see Golden running for his car. I bolted toward the men on the bridge. They had stopped working and were gawking at the strange man who was heading for them. I yelled, "Get down. That man's got a gun. Call the police."

The four guys headed for cover behind the equipment and large wooden crates on one side of the bridge. I caught a brief glimpse of one of them talking into a cell phone, as I plowed toward them as fast as I could.

"Hold it, Tom. I don't want to shoot you, but I will if you don't stop."

Somehow, Nate had beaten me to the bridge. Without a moment's hesitation, I threw myself over the railing. I had decided in a split second that I'd rather be killed by a fall into Yaquina Bay hundreds of feet below than be knocked off by a bullet from a friend who had gone crazy.

As I went over the side, I grabbed hold of a rusty girder, which left my feet dangling helplessly in the air. Then, miraculously, one foot hit something solid. I couldn't see in the darkness, but I lowered myself slowly and landed on all fours on a wide, wooden scaffold used by the painters to work under the bridge. It even had a railing. The wind and my abrupt arrival had caused the platform to sway.

"Tom, you stupid son of a bitch." I could just make out Nate Golden leaning over the bridge, gun in hand. Suddenly, a strong light pierced the darkness, skittering by me and focusing on him.

"This is the United States Coast Guard," intoned a man speaking through a bullhorn from a boat below. "Drop your weapon."

Silence from above.

"Drop your weapon," the voice repeated.

I decided to use this opportunity to get up onto the road. While I climbed up and over the railing, Nate remained turned with his back to me—he seemed to be mesmerized by the spotlight. It put him in a trance, and he began to sway back and forth. Then, he suddenly walked to the edge of the bridge and climbed up, ready to jump, his gun still in his hand.

"Nate, it's Tom," I shouted, running toward him. Inexplicably, I had discarded any worries about my own well-being and was thinking only of trying to save a good friend.

He was saying something, but I couldn't hear every word.

"I understand," I shouted. "What happened to your family was a terrible injustice. Don't dishonor their memory with another death."

Golden didn't reply, as I slowed to a hesitant walk toward him. Then I spotted a tiny point of light on his back. A sharpshooter had a bead on him with his electronic nightscope.

"Put your hands up, Nate," I shouted over the rising wind, "or they'll shoot you."

But he ignored my words and stood up, brandishing his gun.

As the bullet pierced Golden's neck, he stood motionless for several seconds. Then, that gentle man who could not escape the demons from the past, careened into the waters of Yaquina Bay.

30

As I rushed to the side of the bridge, the searchlight from the Coast Guard boat was trained on a spot of churning water. Tears streamed down my face as I tried to comprehend the torment that had driven a good man to his death.

I slowly stepped down onto the roadway. All I could think about now was getting away from this horror. But as I looked up, a phalanx of deputies carrying black shields was advancing on me about a hundred yards away.

"Assume the position." The sheriff's voice. I kept walking toward the skirmish line so I could get within shouting distance.

"Martindale. Get down on the ground."

I ignored the ridiculous command and the line halted. Then I heard the unmistakable click of rifles being locked and loaded. I got down on all fours, face down, real fast.

I could hear the clomping of Kutler's boots on the asphalt as he approached. I raised my head slightly. "Sheriff, what's this all about?"

"It looked to me like you were with him—trying to get away."

"Yeah, I was trying to get away from the guy you shot."

"It all looked pretty suspicious to me. Who was that guy, anyway?"

"Nate Golden—that's who you shot," I said, coming to a sitting position.

Kutler gasped. "I don't believe you. It couldn't be—not a police officer," he stammered. Then, regaining his composure, he pulled me to my feet. "I think we need to take you to the courthouse and have ourselves a little talk."

"That won't be necessary, Art," said a familiar voice behind me. "The OSP has jurisdiction. Our man was killed. Mr. Martindale is a material witness to a shooting carried out by you or one of your men. That's who will be coming to our office for questioning."

Angela Pride never sounded more authoritative and in charge. We exchanged quick smiles as I walked toward her. She was accompanied by two other state police officers.

"Nate Golden is our man, Art, and we need to set this right. I'll keep you fully informed of our progress. For now, let's move on. We've got traffic backed up for miles in both directions."

After I made a detailed statement to a state police investigator at the Newport office, Angela drove me home, telling the others it was on her way. She had promised to fill in the blanks of the story that had consumed my life for the past week.

Once inside, I took a hot shower to warm up, then joined Angela at the kitchen table. She set a cup of steaming coffee and a Spanish omelet before me.

"That looks good. Thanks for saving me once again. I hope you never get tired of doing that."

"If you'd stick to your books and writing paper, I wouldn't have to come to your rescue so often." She wasn't smiling. "I'd suggest a permanent move to another county. Art Kutler is not going to forget how you humiliated him tonight. If you so much as have a dirty car, he's going to give you a ticket."

"Maybe I can hang on until he retires. Next summer I'll stay locked in this house for three months. You'd bring me food and other sustaining things, wouldn't you, Angela?"

I smiled, but she didn't. "We'll cross that bridge when we come to it, Tom."

"Did you say bridge or bed?"

She laughed.

"Tell me about Nate," I said.

"This is strictly between us. Headquarters in Salem is handling the media on this. It's pretty hard to explain why a cop goes bad."

"It had to do with his family and the war."

"Yes, it did. He said that in a note to you."

"Note? He left me a note?"

"I have a copy here for you. We kept the original for evidence. While you were making your statement, we went to his apartment. It was propped up on his desk marked 'In the event of my death'."

I reached for my glasses and began to read.

> *Hello Tom:*
>
> *If you're reading this, I'll be dead. I've done some stupid things while trying to avenge the terrible atrocities that happened to my family. I needed to read your friend's manuscript because I knew those Germans were related to the man who ruined my grandfather's life. I first heard some of it in a literary group we both belonged to. She wouldn't let me read it. She wanted you to see it first. I tried to get it from her, but she hid it. That's why I followed you. I wanted you to lead me to it. That stupid Wright woman wouldn't open her safe. She just tried to seduce me. I had to read those pages.*

Along the way, I became afraid you would find me out.
I'm sorry. I couldn't let anyone stop me in my mission.
Forgive me.
      Nate

I looked up at Angela and took off my glasses. "He fancied himself on a mission to kill Nazis?"

"There were all kinds of things on the French Resistance in his apartment. We think he actually became his grandfather in his mind. He was really fighting World War II all over again, especially after he found out that Bader and his cousin were related to the Nazi officer who murdered his family."

"But how? He apparently heard Simone read only a small portion in the literary group."

"That caught his interest, and then he went looking for more details. We found some material from the Holocaust Research Center in L.A. They helped track the information down."

"I got some material from there, too. That's how I found out that Nate was related to someone in a French town near where Simone lived. What I don't understand is why Nate was so determined to read her memoir that he would kill her to get ahold of it. Didn't he already know who the Germans were?"

"Probably, but I guess he wanted to confirm it. Police personnel are trained to check out everything more than once. We think he was watching Simone and followed her to the lighthouse and tried to talk her into giving him the manuscript."

"Why didn't she?"

"You knew her, Tom. Sounds like she was plucky enough to refuse him."

"That would be Simone. She was pretty feisty," I said.

"When she wouldn't let him see it, Nate probably got frustrated, they struggled, and he killed her with Adam Edwards's spade. He must have anticipated everything and brought it along in case he needed it to frame poor Edwards."

"My God, think of all the preparations he had to make in advance, in case things didn't go his way."

"Obsession does that. We don't know the whole story, but he made sure all evidence of the break-in at Simone's house and Connie Wright's murder was handled by him. He could get rid of his fingerprints that way."

"What about Connie?"

"Another older lady who stood in his way. She was vulnerable because she couldn't resist a good-looking man, even if it killed her."

"Poor Connie," I said, shaking my head.

"And Nate was the one who broke into Simone's house and put the Nazi swastika on her computer?"

"I think so. To set the Germans up as suspects."

"So they're completely in the clear?"

"They're only guilty of having a nasty relative."

"But why go after Adam?"

"I think Nate was afraid Adam saw him kill Simone at the lighthouse."

"What about Adam?" I asked, suddenly remembering his mother.

"He's fine. Rose has taken him to Eugene."

"He's a real survivor, that guy," I said, shaking my head. "How about the lawyer and the mortician I told you about?"

"Just two guys with an eye for prime coastal property."

"And Chuck Gates?"

"He might have seen Nate at Connie Wright's house, but I don't think Nate saw him. I'm not sure how he found out about Simone Godard. Maybe he just guessed. We found records in his trailer about the surveillance he was conducting on you. He was as obsessed with you as Nate was with the Germans. What he was really interested in was causing as much trouble as he could for you, whenever or wherever he could. We also found a lot of material about the aquarium and the new marine mammal exhibit. He had highlighted some stuff about a shark with one blind eye."

"I'll never forget that nasty little encounter," I said, smiling weakly.

Angela stood up and started clearing the table, then she looked at her watch. "It's nearly seven. I'll call you in a few days after I've sorted out all this Golden mess. Maybe I can come over next weekend."

"I'd love that," I said.

After Angela left, I walked out my back door and across the yard to the cliff and the sea below. I took several deep breaths of energizing sea-scented air and thought how good it was to be alive. A seabird cried, and in the distance I caught a glimpse of the Yaquina Head Lighthouse. That symbol of endurance and safe haven was strangely reassuring. As I crossed the yard and walked back into the house, I was glad not to be thinking about ancient horror and recent death for the first time in a long time.